ROBERT SHECKLEY
SHARDS OF SPACE

Man is resourceful, right? But pit him against:

—the last five surviving women on Earth
—a computer-coordinated galactic invading army
—the Earth-takeover bid of a meddling Martian bug

ELEVEN SPACED-OUT STORIES ABOUT
MEN IN THEIR ETERNAL STRUGGLE
TO DOMINATE THE UNIVERSE

Bantam Books by Robert Sheckley

CALIBRE .50
DEAD RUN
IMMORTALITY, INC.
LIVE GOLD
NOTIONS: UNLIMITED
PILGRIMAGE TO EARTH
SHARDS OF SPACE
STORE OF INFINITY
TIME LIMIT
WHITE DEATH

shards
of space

robert
sheckley

A NATIONAL GENERAL COMPANY

SHARDS OF SPACE
A Bantam Book / published July 1962
2nd printing .... February 1971

ACKNOWLEDGMENTS

"Alone at Last" originally appeared in INFINITY *Magazine. Copyright 1956, by Royal Publications, Inc.*

"Fool's Mate" originally appeared in ASTOUNDING SCIENCE FICTION *Magazine March 1953. Copyright 1953, by Astounding Science Fiction Magazine.*

"Forever" originally appeared in GALAXY *Magazine February 1953. Copyright 1953, by Galaxy Publishing Corporation.*

"The Girls and Nugent Miller" originally appeared in THE MAGAZINE OF FANTASY AND SCIENCE FICTION *March 1960. Copyright 1960, by Mercury Press, Inc.*

"Meeting of the Minds" originally appeared in GALAXY *Magazine February 1960. Copyright 1960, by Galaxy Publishing Corporation.*

"Potential" originally appeared in ASTOUNDING SCIENCE FICTION *Magazine November 1953. Copyright 1953, by Astounding Science Fiction Magazine.*

"Prospector's Special" originally appeared in GALAXY *Magazine December 1959. Copyright 1959, by Galaxy Publishing Corporation.*

"The Slow Season" originally appeared in THE MAGAZINE OF FANTASY AND SCIENCE FICTION *October 1954. Copyright 1954, by Mercury Press, Inc.*

"The Special Exhibit" originally appeared in ESQUIRE *Magazine October 1953. Copyright 1953, by Esquire, Inc.*

"Subsistence Level" originally appeared in GALAXY *Magazine August 1954. Copyright 1954, by Galaxy Publishing Corporation.*

"The Sweeper of Loray" originally appeared in GALAXY *Magazine April 1959. Copyright 1959, by Galaxy Publishing Corporation.*

Bantam Books are published by Bantam Books, Inc., a National General company. Its trade-mark, consisting of the words "Bantam Books" and the portrayal of a bantam is registered in the United States Patent Office and in other countries. Marca Registrada. Bantam Books, Inc., 666 Fifth Avenue, New York, N.Y. 10019.

TO MY PARENTS

CONTENTS

PROSPECTOR'S

SPECIAL

THE sandcar moved smoothly over the rolling dunes, its six fat wheels rising and falling like the ponderous rumps of tandem elephants. The hidden sun beat down from a dead-white sky, pouring heat into the canvas top, reflecting heat back from the parched sand.

"Stay awake," Morrison told himself, pulling the sandcar back to its compass course.

It was his twenty-first day on Venus's Scorpion Desert, his twenty-first day of fighting sleep while the sandcar rocked across the dunes, forging over humpbacked little waves. Night travel would have been easier, but there were too many steep ravines to avoid, too many house-sized boulders to dodge. Now he knew why men went into the desert in teams; one man drove while the other kept shaking him awake.

"But it's better alone," Morrison reminded himself. "Half the supplies and no accidental murders."

His head was beginning to droop; he snapped himself erect. In front of him, the landscape shimmered and danced through the polaroid windshield. The sandcar lurched and rocked with treacherous gentleness. Morrison rubbed his eyes and turned on the radio.

He was a big, sunburned, rangy young man with close-cropped black hair and gray eyes. He had come to Venus with a grubstake of twenty thousand dollars, to find his fortune in the Scorpion Desert as others had done before him. He had outfitted in Presto, the last town on the edge of the

1

wilderness, and spent all but ten dollars on the sandcar and equipment.

In Presto, ten dollars just covered the cost of a drink in the town's only saloon. So Morrison ordered rye and water, drank with the miners and prospectors, and laughed at the oldtimers' yarns about the sandwolf packs and the squadrons of voracious birds that inhabited the interior desert. He knew all about sunblindness, heatstroke and telephone breakdown. He was sure none of it would happen to him.

But now, after twenty-one days and eighteen hundred miles, he had learned respect for this waterless waste of sand and stone three times the area of the Sahara. You really *could* die here!

But you could also get rich, and that was what Morrison planned to do.

His radio hummed. At full volume, he could hear the faintest murmur of dance music from Venusborg. Then it faded and only the hum was left.

He turned off the radio and gripped the steering wheel tightly in both hands. He unclenched one hand and looked at his watch. Nine-fifteen in the morning. At ten-thirty he would stop and take a nap. A man had to have rest in this heat. But only a half-hour nap. Treasure lay somewhere ahead of him, and he wanted to find it before his supplies got much lower.

The precious outcroppings of goldenstone *had* to be up ahead! He'd been following traces for two days now. Maybe he would hit a real bonanza, as Kirk did in '89, or Edmonson and Arsler in '93. If so, he would do just what they did. He'd order up a Prospector's Special, and to hell with the cost.

The sandcar rolled along at an even thirty miles an hour, and Morrison tried to concentrate on the heat-blasted yellow-brown landscape. That sandstone patch over there was just the tawny color of Janie's hair.

After he struck it rich, he and Janie would get married, and he'd go back to Earth and buy an ocean farm. No more prospecting. Just one rich strike so he could buy his spread on the deep blue Atlantic. Maybe some people thought fish-herding was tame; it was good enough for him.

He could see it now, the mackerel herds drifting along and browsing at the plankton pens, himself and his trusty dolphin keeping an eye out for the silvery flash of a predatory barracuda or a steel-gray shark coming along behind the branching coral. . . .

Morrison felt the sandcar lurch. He woke up, grabbed the steering wheel and turned it hard. During his moments of sleep, the vehicle had crept over the dune's crumbling edge. Sand and pebbles spun under the fat tires as the sandcar fought for traction. The car tilted perilously. The tires shrieked against the sand, gripped, and started to pull the vehicle back up the slope.

Then the whole face of the dune collapsed.

Morrison held onto the steering wheel as the sandcar flipped over on its side and rolled down the slope. Sand filled his mouth and eyes. He spat and held on while the car rolled over again and dropped into emptiness.

For seconds, he was in the air. The sandcar hit bottom squarely on its wheels. Morrison heard a double boom as the two rear tires blew out. Then his head hit the windshield.

When he recovered consciousness, the first thing he did was look at his watch. It read 10:35.

"Time for that nap," Morrison said to himself. "But I guess I'll survey the situation first."

He found that he was at the bottom of a shallow fault strewn with knife-edged pebbles. Two tires had blown on impact, his windshield was gone, and one of the doors was sprung. His equipment was strewn around, but appeared to be intact.

"Could have been worse," Morrison said.

He bent down to examine the tires more carefully.

"It *is* worse," he said.

The two blown tires were shredded beyond repair. There wasn't enough rubber left in them to make a child's balloon. He had used up his spares ten days back crossing Devil's Grill. Used them and discarded them. He couldn't go on without tires.

Morrison unpacked his telephone. He wiped dust from its black plastic face, then dialed Al's Garage in Presto. After a moment, the small video screen lighted up. He could see a man's long, mournful, grease-stained face.

"Al's Garage. Eddie speaking."

"Hi, Eddie. This is Tom Morrison. I bought that GM sandcar from you about a month ago. Remember?"

"Sure I remember you," Eddie said. "You're the guy doing

a single into the Southwest Track. How's the bus holding out?"

"Fine. Great little car. Reason I called—"

"Hey," Eddie said, "what happened to your face?"

Morrison put his hand to his forehead and felt blood. "Nothing much," he said. "I went over a dune and blew out two tires."

He turned the telephone so that Eddie could see the tires.

"Unrepairable," said Eddie.

"I thought so. And I used up all my spares crossing Devil's Grill. Look, Eddie, I'd like you to 'port me a couple of tires. Retreads are fine. I can't move the sandcar without them."

"Sure," Eddie said, "except I haven't any retreads. I'll have to 'port you new ones at five hundred apiece. Plus four hundred dollars 'porting charges. Fourteen hundred dollars, Mr. Morrison."

"All right."

"Yes, sir. Now if you'll show me the cash, or a money order which you can send back with the receipt, I'll get moving on it."

"At the moment," Morrison said, "I haven't got a cent on me."

"Bank account?"

"Stripped clean."

"Bonds? Property? Anything you can convert into cash?"

"Nothing except this sandcar, which you sold me for eight thousand dollars. When I come back, I'll settle my bill with the sandcar."

"*If* you get back. Sorry, Mr. Morrison. No can do."

"What do you mean?" Morrison asked. "You know I'll pay for the tires."

"And you know the rules on Venus," Eddie said, his mournful face set in obstinate lines. "No credit! Cash and carry!"

"I can't run the sandcar without tires," Morrison said. "Are you going to strand me out here?"

"Who in hell is stranding you?" Eddie asked. "This sort of thing happens to prospectors every day. You know what you have to do now, Mr. Morrison. Call Public Utility and declare yourself a bankrupt. Sign over what's left of the sandcar, equipment, and anything you've found on the way. They'll get you out."

"I'm not turning back," Morrison said. "Look!" He held the telephone close to the ground. "You see the traces,

Eddie? See those red and purple flecks? There's precious stuff near here!"

"Every prospector sees traces," Eddie said. "Damned desert is full of traces."

"These are rich," Morrison said. "These are leading straight to big stuff, a bonanza lode. Eddie, I know it's a lot to ask, but if you could stake me to a couple of tires—"

"I can't do it," Eddie said. "I just work here. I can't 'port you any tires, not unless you show me money first. Otherwise I get fired and probably jailed. You know the law."

"Cash and carry," Morrison said bleakly.

"Right. Be smart and turn back now. Maybe you can try again some other time."

"I spent twelve years getting this stake together," Morrison said. "I'm not going back."

He turned off the telephone and tried to think. Was there anyone else on Venus he could call? Only Max Krandall, his jewel broker. But Max couldn't raise fourteen hundred dollars in that crummy two-by-four office near Venusborg's jewel market. Max could barely scrape up his own rent, much less take care of stranded prospectors.

"I can't ask Max for help," Morrison decided. "Not until I've found goldenstone. The real stuff, not just traces. So that leaves it up to me."

He opened the back of the sandcar and began to unload, piling his equipment on the sand. He would have to choose carefully; anything he took would have to be carried on his back.

The telephone had to go with him, and his lightweight testing kit. Food concentrates, revolver, compass. And nothing else but water, all the water he could carry. The rest of the stuff would have to stay behind.

By nightfall, Morrison was ready. He looked regretfully at the twenty cans of water he was leaving. In the desert, water was a man's most precious possession, second only to his telephone. But it couldn't be helped. After drinking his fill, he hoisted his pack and set a southwest course into the desert.

For three days he trekked to the southwest; then on the fourth day he veered to due south, following an increasingly rich trace. The sun, eternally hidden, beat down on him, and the dead-white sky was like a roof of heated iron over his head. Morrison followed the traces, and something followed him.

On the sixth day, he sensed movement just out of the range of his vision. On the seventh day, he saw what was trailing him.

Venus's own brand of wolf, small, lean, with a yellow coat and long, grinning jaws, it was one of the few mammals that made its home in the Scorpion Desert. As Morrison watched, two more sandwolves appeared beside it.

He loosened the revolver in its holster. The wolves made no attempt to come closer. They had plenty of time.

Morrison kept on going, wishing he had brought a rifle with him. But that would have meant eight pounds more, which meant eight pounds less water.

As he was pitching camp at dusk the eighth day, he heard a crackling sound. He whirled around and located its source, about ten feet to his left and above his head. A little vortex had appeared, a tiny mouth in the air like a whirlpool in the sea. It spun, making the characteristic crackling sounds of 'porting.

"Now who could be 'porting anything to me?" Morrison asked, waiting while the whirlpool slowly widened.

Solidoporting from a base projector to a field target was a standard means of moving goods across the vast distances of Venus. Any inanimate object could be 'ported; animate beings couldn't because the process involved certain minor but distressing molecular changes in protoplasm. A few people had found this out the hard way when 'porting was first introduced.

Morrison waited. The aerial whirlpool became a mouth three feet in diameter. From the mouth stepped a chrome-plated robot carrying a large sack.

"Oh, it's you," Morrison said.

"Yes, sir," the robot said, now completely clear of the field. "Williams Four at your service with the Venus Mail."

It was a robot of medium height, thin-shanked and flat-footed, humanoid in appearance, amiable in disposition. For twenty-three years it had been Venus's entire postal service—sorter, deliverer, and dead storage. It had been built to last, and for twenty-three years the mails had always come through.

"Here we are, Mr. Morrison," Williams 4 said. "Only twice-a-month mail call in the desert, I'm sorry to say, but it comes promptly and that's a blessing. This is for you. And this. I think there's one more. Sandcar broke down, eh?"

"It sure did," Morrison said, taking his letters.

Williams 4 went on rummaging through its bag. Although it was a superbly efficient postman, the old robot was known as the worst gossip on three planets.

"There's one more in here somewhere," Williams 4 said. "Too bad about the sandcar. They just don't build 'em like they did in my youth. Take my advice, young man. Turn back if you still have the chance."

Morrison shook his head.

"Foolish, downright foolish," the old robot said. "Pity you don't have my perspective. Too many's the time I've come across you boys lying in the sand in the dried-out sack of your skin, or with your bones gnawed to splinters by the sandwolves and the filthy black kites. Twenty-three years I've been delivering mail to fine-looking young men like you, and each one thinking he's unique and different."

The robot's eyecells became distant with memory. "But they *aren't* different," Williams 4 said. "They're as alike as robots off the assembly line—especially after the wolves get through with them. And then I have to send their letters and personal effects back to their loved ones on Earth."

"I know," Morrison said. "But some get through, don't they?"

"Sure they do," the robot said. "I've seen men make one, two, three fortunes. And then die on the sands trying to make a fourth."

"Not me," Morrison said. "I just want one. Then I'm going to buy me an undersea farm on Earth."

The robot shuddered. "I have a dread of salt water. But to each his own. Good luck, young man."

The robot looked Morrison over carefully—probably to see what he had in the way of personal effects—then climbed back into the aerial whirlpool. In a moment, it was gone. In another moment, the whirlpool had vanished.

Morrison sat down to read his mail. The first letter was from his jewel broker, Max Krandall. It told about the depression that had hit Venusborg, and hinted that Krandall might have to go into bankruptcy if some of his prospectors didn't strike something good.

The second letter was a statement from the Venus Telephone Company. Morrison owed two hundred and ten dollars and eight cents for two months' telephone service. Unless he remitted this sum at once, his telephone was liable to be turned off.

The last letter, all the way from Earth, was from Janie. It was filled with news about his cousins, aunts and uncles. She told him about the Atlantic farm sites she had looked over, and the wonderful little place she had found near Martinique in the Caribbean. She begged him to give up prospecting if it looked dangerous; they could find another way of financing the farm. She sent all her love and wished him a happy birthday in advance.

"Birthday?" Morrison asked himself. "Let's see, today is July twenty-third. No, it's the twenty-fourth, and my birthday's August first. Thanks for remembering, Janie."

That night he dreamed of Earth and the blue expanse of the Atlantic Ocean. But toward dawn, when the heat of Venus became insistent, he found he was dreaming of mile upon mile of goldenstone, of grinning sandwolves, and of the Prospector's Special.

Rock gave way to sand as Morrison plowed his way across the bottom of a long-vanished lake. Then it was rock again, twisted and tortured into a thousand gaunt shapes. Reds, yellows and browns swam in front of his eyes. In all that desert, there wasn't one patch of green.

He continued his trek into the tumbled stone mazes of the interior desert, and the wolves trekked with him, keeping pace far out on either flank.

Morrison ignored them. He had enough on his mind just to negotiate the sheer cliffs and the fields of broken stone that blocked his way to the south.

By the eleventh day after leaving the sandcar, the traces were almost rich enough for panning. The sandwolves were tracking him still, and his water was almost gone. Another day's march would finish him.

Morrison thought for a moment, then unstrapped his telephone and dialed Public Utility in Venusborg.

The video screen showed a stern, severely dressed woman with iron-gray hair. "Public Utility," she said. "May we be of service?"

"Hi," Morrison said cheerfully. "How's the weather in Venusborg?"

"Hot," the woman said. "How's it out there?"

"I hadn't even noticed," Morrison said, grinning. "Too busy counting my fortune."

"You've found goldenstone?" the woman asked, her expression becoming less severe.

"Sure have," Morrison said. "But don't pass the word

around yet. I'm still staking my claim. I think I can use a refill on these."

Smiling easily, he held up his canteens. Sometimes it worked. Sometimes, if you showed enough confidence, Public Utility would fill you up without checking your account. True, it was embezzling, but this was no time for niceties.

"I suppose your account is in order?" asked the woman.

"Of course," Morrison said, feeling his smile grow stiff. "The name's Tom Morrison. You can just check—"

"Oh, I don't do that personally," the woman said. "Hold that canteen steady. Here we go."

Gripping the canteen in both hands, Morrison watched as the water, 'ported four thousand miles from Venusborg, appeared as a slender crystal stream above the mouth of his canteen. The stream entered the canteen, making a wonderful gurgling sound. Watching it, Morrison found his dry mouth actually was beginning to salivate.

Then the water stopped.

"What's the matter?" Morrison asked.

His video screen went blank. Then it cleared, and Morrison found himself staring into a man's narrow face. The man was seated in front of a large desk. The sign in front of him read *Milton P. Reade, Vice President, Accounts*.

"Mr. Morrison," Reade said, "your account is overdrawn. You have been obtaining water under false pretenses. That is a criminal offense."

"I'm going to pay for the water," Morrison said.

"When?"

"As soon as I get back to Venusborg."

"With what," asked Mr. Reade, "do you propose to pay?"

"With goldenstone," Morrison said. "Look around here, Mr. Reade. The traces are rich! Richer than they were for the Kirk claim! I'll be hitting the outcroppings in another day—"

"That's what every prospector thinks," Mr. Reade said. "Every prospector on Venus is only a day from goldenstone. And they all expect credit from Public Utility."

"But in this case—"

"Public Utility," Mr. Reade continued inexorably, "is not a philanthropic organization. Its charter specifically forbids the extension of credit. Venus is a frontier, Mr. Morrison, a *farflung* frontier. Every manufactured article on Venus must be imported from Earth at outrageous cost. We do have our own water, but locating it, purifying it, then 'porting it is an expensive process. This company, like every other company on Venus, necessarily operates on a very narrow margin of profit, which is invariably plowed back into further expansion. That is why there can be no credit on Venus."

"I know all that," Morrison said. "But I'm telling you, I only need a day or two more—"

"Absolutely impossible. By the rules, we shouldn't even help you out now. The time to report bankruptcy was a week ago, when your sandcar broke down. Your garage man reported, as required by law. But you didn't. We would be within our rights to leave you stranded. Do you understand that?"

"Yes, of course," Morrison said wearily.

"However, the company has decided to stretch a point in your favor. If you turn back immediately, we will keep you supplied with water for the return trip."

"I'm not turning back yet. I'm almost on the real stuff."

"You must turn back! Be reasonable, Morrison! Where would we be if we let every prospector wander over the desert while we supplied his water? There'd be ten thousand men out there, and we'd be out of business inside of a year. I'm stretching the rules now. Turn back."

"No," said Morrison.

"You'd better think about it. If you don't turn back now, Public Utility takes no further responsibility for your water supply."

Morrison nodded. If he went on, he would stand a good chance of dying in the desert. But if he turned back, what then? He would be in Venusborg, penniless and in debt, looking for work in an overcrowded city. He'd sleep in a community shed and eat at a soup kitchen with the other prospectors who had turned back. And how would he be able to raise the fare back to Earth? When would he ever see Janie again?

"I guess I'll keep on going," Morrison said.

"Then Public Utility takes no further responsibility for you," Reade repeated, and hung up.

Morrison packed up his telephone, took a sip from his meager water supply, and went on.

The sandwolves loped along at each side, moving in closer. Overhead, a delta-winged kite found him. It balanced on the updrafts for a day and a night, waiting for the wolves to finish him. Then a flock of small flying scorpions sighted the waiting kite. They drove the big creature upstairs into the cloud bank. For a day the flying reptiles waited. Then they in turn were driven off by a squadron of black kites.

The traces were very rich now, on the fifteenth day since he had left the sandcar. By rights, he should be walking over goldenstone. He should be surrounded by goldenstone. But still he hadn't found any.

Morrison sat down and shook his last canteen. It gave off no wet sound. He uncapped it and turned it up over his mouth. Two drops trickled down his parched throat.

It was about four days since he had talked to Public Utility. He must have used up the last of his water yesterday. Or had it been the day before?

He recapped the empty canteen and looked around at the heat-blasted landscape. Abruptly he pulled the telephone out of his pack and dialed Max Krandall in Venusborg.

Krandall's round, worried face swam into focus on the screen. "Tommy," he said, "you look like hell."

"I'm all right," Morrison said. "A little dried out, that's all. Max, I'm near goldenstone."

"Are you sure?" Krandall asked.

"See for yourself," Morrison said, swinging the telephone around. "Look at the stone formations! Do you see the red and purple markings over there?"

"Traces, all right," Krandall admitted dubiously.

"There's rich stuff just beyond it," Morrison said. "There has to be! Look, Max, I know you're short on money, but I'm going to ask you a favor. Send me a pint of water. Just a pint, so I can go on for another day or two. We can both get rich for the price of a pint of water."

"I can't do it," Krandall said sadly.

"You can't?"

"That's right. Tommy, I'd send you water even if there wasn't anything around you but sandstone and granite. Do you think I'd let you die of thirst if I could help it? But I can't do a thing. Take a look."

Krandall rotated his telephone. Morrison saw that the chairs, table, desk, filing cabinet and safe were gone from the office. All that was left in the room was the telephone.

"I don't know why they haven't taken out the phone," Krandall said. "I owe two months on my bill."

"I do too," said Morrison.

"I'm stripped," Krandall said. "I haven't got a dime. Don't get me wrong, I'm not worried about myself. I can always eat at a soup kitchen. But I can't 'port you any water. Not you or Remstaater."

"Jim Remstaater?"

"Yeah. He was following a trace up north past Forgotten River. His sandcar broke an axle last week and he wouldn't turn back. His water ran out yesterday."

"I'd bail him out if I could," said Morrison.

"And he'd bail you out if he could," Krandall said. "But he can't and you can't and I can't. Tommy, you have only one hope."

"What's that?"

"Find goldenstone. Not just traces, find the real thing worth real money. Then phone me. If you really have goldenstone, I'll bring in Wilkes from Tri-Planet Mining and get him to advance us some money. He'll probably want fifty per cent of the claim."

"That's plain robbery!"

"No, it's just the high cost of credit on Venus," Krandall answered. "Don't worry, there'll still be plenty left over. But you have to find goldenstone first."

"OK," Morrison said. "It should be around here somewhere. Max, what's today's date?"

"July thirty-first. Why?"

"Just wondering. I'll call you when I've found something."

After hanging up, Morrison sat on a little boulder and stared dully at the sand. July thirty-first. Tomorrow was his birthday. His family would be thinking about him. Aunt Bess in Pasadena, the twins in Laos, Uncle Ted in Durango. And Janie, of course, waiting for him in Tampa.

Morrison realized that tomorrow might be his last birthday unless he found goldenstone.

He got to his feet, strapped the telephone back in his pack beside the empty canteens, and set a course to the south.

He wasn't alone. The birds and beasts of the desert marched with him. Overhead, the silent black kites circled endlessly. The sandwolves crept closer on his flanks, their red tongues lolling out, waiting for the carcass to fall . . .

"I'm not dead yet!" Morrison shouted at them.

He drew his revolver and fired at the nearest wolf. At twenty feet, he missed. He went down on one knee, held the revolver tightly in both hands and fired again. The wolf yelped in pain. The pack immediately went for the wounded animal, and the kites swooped down for their share.

Morrison put the revolver back in its holster and went on.

He could tell he was in a badly dehydrated state. The landscape jumped and danced in front of him, and his footing was unsure. He discarded the empty canteens, threw away everything but the testing kit, telephone and revolver. Either he was coming out of the desert in style or he wasn't coming out at all.

The traces continued to run rich. But still he came upon no sign of tangible wealth.

That evening he found a shallow cave set into the base of a cliff. He crawled inside and built a barricade of rocks across the entrance. Then he drew his revolver and leaned back against the far wall.

The sandwolves were outside, sniffing and snapping their jaws. Morrison propped himself up and got ready for an all-night vigil.

He didn't sleep, but he couldn't stay awake, either. Dreams and visions tormented him. He was back on Earth and Janie was saying to him, "It's the tuna. Something must be wrong with their diet. Every last one of them is sick."

"It's the darnedest thing," Morrison told her. "Just as soon as you domesticate a fish, it turns into a prima donna."

"Are you going to stand there philosophizing," Janie asked, "while your fish are sick?"

"Call the vet."

"I did. He's off at the Blake's place, taking care of their dairy whale."

"All right, I'll go out and take a look." He slipped on his face mask. Grinning, he said, "I don't even have time to dry off before I have to go out again."

His face and chest were wet.

Morrison opened his eyes. His face and chest *were* wet —from perspiration. Staring at the partially blocked mouth of the cave, he could see green eyes, two, four, six, eight.

He fired at them, but they didn't retreat. He fired again, and his bullet ricocheted off the cave wall, stinging him with stone splinters. With his next shots, he succeeded in winging one of the wolves. The pack withdrew.

That emptied the revolver. Morrison searched through his pockets and found five more cartridges. He carefully loaded the gun. Dawn couldn't be far away now.

And then he was dreaming again, this time of the Prospector's Special. He had heard about it in every little saloon that bordered the Scorpion. Bristly-bearded old prospectors told a hundred different stories about it, and the cynical bartenders chimed in with their versions. Kirk had it in '89, ordered up big and special just for him. Edmonson and Arsler received it in '93. That was certain. And other men had had it too, as they sat on their precious goldenstone claims. Or so people said.

But was it real? Was there such a thing as the Prospector's Special? Would he live to see that rainbow-hued wonder, tall as a church steeple, wide as a house, more precious than goldenstone itself?

Sure he would! Why, he could almost see it now . . .

Morrison shook himself awake. It was morning. Painfully, he crawled out of the cave to face the day.

He stumbled and crawled to the south, escorted closely by wolves, shaded by predatory flying things. His fingers scrabbled along rock and sand. The traces were rich, rich!

But where in all this desolation was the goldenstone?

Where? He was almost past caring. He drove his sunburned, dried-out body, stopping only to fire a single shot when the wolves came too close.

Four bullets left.

He had to fire again when the kites, growing impatient, started diving at his head. A lucky shot tore into the flock, downing two. It gave the wolves something to fight over. Morrison crawled on blindly.

And fell over the edge of a little cliff.

It wasn't a serious fall, but the revolver was knocked from his hand. Before he could find it, the wolves were on him. Only their greed saved Morrison. While they fought over him, he rolled away and retrieved his revolver. Two shots scattered the pack. That left one bullet.

He'd have to save that one for himself, because he was too tired to go on. He sank to his knees. The traces were rich here. Fantastically rich. Somewhere nearby . . .

"Well, I'll be damned," Morrison said.

The little ravine into which he had fallen was solid goldenstone.

He picked up a pebble. Even in its rough state he could see the deep luminous golden glow, the fiery red and purple flecks deep in the shining stone.

"Make sure," Morrison told himself. "No false alarms, no visions, no wild hopes. Make sure."

He broke off a chunk of rock with the butt of his revolver. It still looked like goldenstone. He took out his testing kit and spilled a few drops of white solution on the rock. The solution foamed green.

"Goldenstone, sure as sure," Morrison said, looking around at the glowing cliff walls. "Hey, I'm rich!"

He took out his telephone. With trembling fingers he dialed Krandall's number.

"Max!" Morrison shouted. "I've hit it! I've hit the real stuff!"

"My name is not Max," a voice over the telephone said.

"Huh?"

"My name is Boyard," the man said.

The video screen cleared, and Morrison saw a thin, sallow-faced man with a hairline mustache.

"I'm sorry, Mr. Boyard," Morrison said. "I must have gotten the wrong number. I was calling—"

"It doesn't matter who you were calling," Mr. Boyard said. "I am District Supervisor of the Venus Telephone Company. Your bill is two months overdue."

"I can pay it now," Morrison said, grinning.

"Excellent," said Mr. Boyard. "As soon as you do, your service will be resumed."

The screen began to fade.

"Wait!" Morrison cried. "I can pay as soon as I reach your office. But I must make one telephone call. Just one call, so that I—"

"Not a chance," Mr. Boyard said decisively. "*After* you have paid your bill, your service will be turned on immediately."

"I've got the money right here!" Morrison said. "Right here in my hand!"

Mr. Boyard paused. "Well, it's unusual, but I suppose we could arrange for a special robot messenger if you are willing to pay the expenses."

"I am!"

"Hm. It's irregular, but I daresay we . . . Where is the money?"

"Right here," Morrison said. "You recognize it, don't you? It's goldenstone!"

"I am sick and tired of the tricks you prospectors think you can put over on us. Holding up a handful of pebbles—"

"But this is really goldenstone! Can't you see it?"

"I am a businessman," Mr. Boyard said, "not a jeweler. I wouldn't know goldenstone from goldenrod."

The video screen went blank.

Frantically, Morrison tried to reach the operator. There was nothing, not even a dial tone. His telephone was disconnected.

He put the instrument down and surveyed his situation. The narrow crevice into which he had fallen ran straight for about twenty yards, then curved to the left. No cave was visible in the steep walls, no place where he could build a barricade.

He heard a movement behind him. Whirling around, he saw a huge old wolf in full charge. Without a moment's hesitation, Morrison drew and fired, blasting off the top of the beast's head.

"Damn it," Morrison said. "I was going to save that bullet for myself."

It gave him a moment's grace. He ran down the ravine, looking for an opening in its sides. Goldenstone glowed at him and sparkled red and purple. And the sandwolves loped along behind him.

Then Morrison stopped. In front of him, the curving ravine ended in a sheer wall.

He put his back against it, holding the revolver by its butt. The wolves stopped five feet from him, gathering themselves for a rush. There were ten or twelve of them, and they were packed three deep in the narrow pass. Overhead, the kites circled, waiting for their turn.

At that moment, Morrison heard the crackling sound of 'porting equipment. A whirlpool appeared above the wolves' heads and they backed hastily away.

"Just in time!" Morrison said.

"In time for what?" asked Williams 4, the postman.

The robot climbed out of the vortex and looked around.

"Well, young man," Williams 4 said, "this is a fine fix you've gotten yourself into. Didn't I warn you? Didn't I advise you to turn back? And now look!"

"You were perfectly right," Morrison said. "What did Max Krandall send me?"

"Max Krandall did not, and could not, send a thing."

"Then why are you here?"

"Because it's your birthday," Williams 4 said. "We of the Postal Department always give special service for birthdays. Here you are."

Williams 4 gave him a handful of mail, birthday greetings from Janie, and from his aunts, uncles and cousins on Earth.

"Something else here," Williams 4 said, rummaging in his

bag. "I *think* there was something else here. Let me see . . . Yes, here it is."

He handed Morrison a small package.

Hastily, Morrison tore off the wrappings. It was a birthday present from his Aunt Mina in New Jersey. He opened it. It was a large box of salt-water taffy, direct from Atlantic City.

"Quite a delicacy, I'm told," said Williams 4, who had been peering over his shoulder. "But not very satisfactory under the circumstances. Well, young man, I hate to see anyone die on his birthday. The best I can wish you is a speedy and painless departure."

The robot began walking toward the vortex.

"Wait!" Morrison cried. "You can't just leave me like this! I haven't had any water in days! And those wolves—"

"I know," Williams 4 said. "Do you think I feel *happy* about it? Even a robot has some feelings!"

"Then help me."

"I can't. The rules of the Postal Department expressly and categorically forbid it. I remember Abner Lathe making much the same request of me in '97. It took three years for a burial party to reach him."

"You have an emergency telephone, haven't you?" Morrison asked.

"Yes. But I can use it only for personal emergencies."

"Can you at least carry a letter for me? A special delivery letter?"

"Of course I can," the robot postman said. "That's what I'm here for. I can even lend you pencil and paper."

Morrison accepted the pencil and paper and tried to think. If he wrote to Max now, special delivery, Max would have the letter in a matter of hours. But how long would Max need to raise some money and send him water and ammunition? A day, two days? Morrison would have to figure out some way of holding out . . .

"I assume you have a stamp," the robot said.

"I don't," Morrison replied. "But I'll buy one from you. Solidoport special."

"Excellent," said the robot. "We have just put out a new series of Venusborg triangulars. I consider them quite an esthetic accomplishment. They cost three dollars apiece."

"That's fine. Very reasonable. Let me have one."

"There is the question of payment."

"Here," Morrison said, handing the robot a piece of golden-stone worth about five thousand dollars in the rough.

The postman examined the stone, then handed it back. "I'm sorry, I can accept only cash."

"But this is worth more than a thousand postage stamps!" Morrison said. "This is goldenstone!"

"It may well be," Williams 4 said. "But I have never had any assaying knowledge taped into me. Nor is the Venus Postal Service run on a barter system. I'll have to ask for three dollars in bills or coins."

"I don't have it."

"I am very sorry." Williams 4 turned to go.

"You can't just go and let me die!"

"I can and must," Williams 4 said sadly. "I am only a robot, Mr. Morrison. I was made by men, and naturally I partake of some of their sensibilities. That's as it should be. But I also have my limits, which, in their nature, are similar to the limits most humans have on this harsh planet. And, unlike humans, I cannot transcend my limits."

The robot started to climb into the whirlpool. Morrison stared at him blankly, and saw beyond him the waiting wolf-pack. He saw the soft glow of several million dollars' worth of goldenstone shining from the ravine's walls.

Something snapped inside him.

With an inarticulate yell, Morrison dived, tackling the robot around the ankles. Williams 4, half in and half out of the 'porting vortex, struggled and kicked, and almost succeeded in shaking Morrison loose. But with a maniac's strength Morrison held on. Inch by inch he dragged the robot out of the vortex, threw him on the ground and pinned him.

"You are disrupting the mail service," said Williams 4.

"That's not all I'm going to disrupt," Morrison growled. "I'm not afraid of dying. That was part of the gamble. But I'm damned if I'm going to die fifteen minutes after I've struck it rich!"

"You have no choice."

"I do. I'm going to use that emergency telephone of yours."

"You can't," Williams 4 said. "I refuse to extrude it. And you could never reach it without the resources of a machine shop."

"Could be," said Morrison. "I plan to find out." He pulled out his empty revolver.

"What are you going to do?" Williams 4 asked.

"I'm going to see if I can smash you into scrap metal *without* the resources of a machine shop. I think your eye-cells would be a logical place to begin."

"They would indeed," said the robot. "I have no personal sense of survival, of course. But let me point out that you would be leaving all Venus without a postman. Many would suffer because of your antisocial action."

"I hope so," Morrison said, raising the revolver above his head.

"Also," the robot said hastily, "you would be destroying government property. That is a serious offense."

Morrison laughed and swung the pistol. The robot moved its head quickly, dodging the blow. It tried to wriggle free, but Morrison's two hundred pounds was seated firmly on its thorax.

"I won't miss this time," Morrison promised, hefting the revolver.

"Stop!" Williams 4 said. "It is my duty to protect government property, even if that property happens to be myself. You may use my telephone, Mr. Morrison. Bear in mind that this offense if punishable by a sentence of not more than ten and not less than five years in the Solar Swamp Penitentiary."

"Let's have that telephone," Morrison said.

The robot's chest opened and a small telephone extruded. Morrison dialed Max Krandall and explained the situation.

"I see, I see," Krandall said. "All right, I'll try to find Wilkes. But, Tom, I don't know how much I can do. It's after business hours. Most places are closed—"

"Get them open again," said Morrison. "I can pay for it. And get Jim Remstaater out of trouble, too."

"It can't be done just like that. You haven't established any rights to your claim. You haven't even proved that your claim is valuable."

"Look at it." Morrison turned the telephone so that Krandall could see the glowing walls of the ravine.

"Looks real," Krandall said. "But unfortunately, all that glitters is not goldenstone."

"What can we do?" Morrison asked.

"We'll have to take it step by step. I'll 'port you the Public Surveyor. He'll check your claim, establish its limits, and make sure no one else has filed on it. You give him a chunk of goldenstone to take back. A big chunk."

"How can I cut goldenstone? I don't have any tools."

"You'll have to figure out a way. He'll take the chunk back for assaying. If it's rich enough, you're all set."

"And if it isn't?"

"Perhaps we better not talk about that," Krandall said. "I'll get right to work on this, Tommy. Good luck!"

Morrison signed off. He stood up and helped the robot to its feet.

"In twenty-three years of service," Williams 4 said, "this is the first time anybody has threatened the life of a government postal employee. I must report this to the police authorities at Venusborg, Mr. Morrison. I have no choice."

"I know," Morrison said. "But I guess five or ten years in the penitentiary is better than dying."

"I doubt it. I carry mail there, you know. You will have the opportunity of seeing for yourself in about six months."

"What?" said Morrison, stunned.

"In about six months, after I have completed my mail calls around the planet and returned to Venusborg. A matter like this must be reported in person. But first and foremost, the mails must go through."

"Thanks, Williams. I don't know how—"

"I am simply performing my duty," the robot said as it climbed into the vortex. "If you are still on Venus in six months, I will be delivering your mail to the penitentiary."

"I won't be here," Morrison said. "So long, Williams!"

The robot disappeared into the 'porting vortex. Then the vortex disappeared. Morrison was alone in the Venusian twilight.

He found an outcropping of goldenstone larger than a man's head. He chipped at it with his pistol butt, and tiny particles danced and shimmered in the air. After an hour, he had put four dents in his revolver, but he had barely scratched the highly refractory surface of the goldenstone.

The sandwolves began to edge forward. Morrison threw stones at them and shouted in his dry, cracked voice. The wolves retreated.

He examined the outcropping again and found a hairline fault running along one edge. He concentrated his blows along the fault.

The goldenstone refused to crack.

Morrison wiped sweat from his eyes and tried to think. A chisel, he needed a chisel . . .

He pulled off his belt. Putting the edge of the steel buckle against the crack, he managed to hammer it in a fraction of an inch. Three more blows drove the buckle firmly into the fault. With another blow, the outcropping sheared off cleanly. He had separated a twenty-pound piece from the cliff. At fifty dollars a troy ounce, this lump should be worth about twelve thousand dollars—if it assayed out as pure as it looked.

The twilight had turned a deep gray when the Public Surveyor 'ported in. It was a short, squat robot with a conservative crackle-black finish.

"Good day, sir," the surveyor said. "You wish to file a claim? A standard unrestricted mining claim?"

"That's right," Morrison said.

"And where is the center of the aforesaid claim?"

"Huh? The center? I guess I'm standing on it."

"Very well," the robot said.

Extruding a steel tape, it walked rapidly away from Morrison. At a distance of two hundred yards, it stopped. More steel tape fluttered as it walked, flew and climbed a square with Morrison at the center. When it had finished, the surveyor stood for a long time without moving.

"What are you doing?" Morrison asked.

"I'm making depth-photographs of the terrain," the robot said. "It's rather difficult in this light. Couldn't you wait till morning?"

"No!"

"Well, I'll just have to cope," the robot said.

It moved and stood, moved and stood, each subterranean exposure taking longer than the last as the twilight deepened. If it had had pores, it would have sweated.

"There," said the robot at last, "that takes care of it. Do you have a sample for me to take back?"

"Here it is," Morrison said, hefting the slab of goldenstone and handing it to the surveyor. "Is that all?"

"Absolutely all," the robot said. "Except, of course, that you haven't given me the Deed of Search."

Morrison blinked. "I haven't given you the what?"

"The Deed of Search. That is a government document showing that the claim you are filing on is free, as per government order, of fissionable material in excess of fifty per cent of the total mass to a depth of sixty feet. It's a mere formality, but a necessary one."

"I never heard of it," Morrison said.

"It became a requirement last week," explained the surveyor. "You don't have the Deed? Then I'm afraid your standard unrestricted claim is invalid."

"Isn't there anything I can do?"

"Well," the robot said, "you *could* change your standard unrestricted claim to a special restricted claim. That requires no Deed of Search."

"What does the special restricted part mean?"

"It means that in five hundred years all rights revert to the Government of Venus."

"All right!" Morrison shouted. "Fine! Good! Is that all?"

"Absolutely all," the surveyor said. "I shall bring this sample back and have it assayed and evaluated immediately. From it and the depth-photographs we can extrapolate the value and extent of your claim."

"Send me back something to take care of the wolves," Morrison said. "And food. And listen—I want a Prospector's Special."

"Yes, sir. It will all be 'ported to you—if your claim is of sufficient value to warrant the outlay."

The robot climbed into the vortex and vanished.

Time passed, and the wolves edged forward again. They snarled at the rocks Morrison threw, but they didn't retreat. Jaws open and tongues lolling, they crept up the remaining yards between them and the prospector.

Then the leading wolf leaped back and howled. A gleaming vortex had appeared over his head and a rifle had fallen from the vortex, striking him on a forepaw.

The wolves scrambled away. Another rifle fell from the vortex. Then a large box marked *Grenades, Handle With Care*. Then another box marked *Desert Ration K*.

Morrison waited, staring at the gleaming mouth of the vortex. It crossed the sky to a spot a quarter of a mile away and paused there, and then a great round brass base emerged from the vortex, and the mouth widened to allow an even greater bulge of brass to which the base was attached. The bulge grew higher as the base was lowered to the sand. When the last of it appeared, it stood alone in the horizon-to-horizon expanse, a gigantic ornate brass punchbowl in the desert. The vortex rose and paused again over the bowl.

Morrison waited, his throat raw and aching. Now a small trickle came out of the vortex and splashed down into the bowl. Still Morrison didn't move.

And then it came. The trickle became a roar that sent the wolves and kites fleeing in terror, and a cataract poured from the vortex to the huge punchbowl.

Morrison began staggering toward it. He should have ordered a canteen, he told himself thirstily, stumbling across the quarter of a mile of sand. But at last he stood beneath the Prospector's Special, higher than a church steeple, wider than a house, filled with water more precious than golden-stone itself. He turned the spigot at the bottom. Water soaked the yellow sands and ran in rivulets down the dune.

He should have ordered a cup or glass, Morrison thought, lying on his back with open mouth.

The Girls and

Nugent Miller

NUGENT MILLER bent
down and examined the footprints, gently brushing aside
leaves and twigs with his pocket knife. They had been made
recently, by a small foot. Perhaps a woman's foot?

Staring at the footprints, Miller could glimpse the woman
rising from them, could see too vividly the high-arched foot,
the narrow ankle and the slender golden legs. Turning the
imaginary woman on her imaginary pedestal, Miller admired
the long graceful curve of her back, and he could see—

"That's enough," he told himself. He had no proof other
than the footprint. Hope could be dangerous, desire could be
catastrophic.

He was a tall, thin, sad-faced man, very sunburned, wearing sneakers, khaki slacks and a blue polo shirt. He had a
knapsack on his back and a geiger counter in his hand. He
wore horn-rimmed glasses. The left sidepiece had been broken
and repaired with a twig and string, and he had reinforced
the nosepiece with wire. The glasses seemed secure now,
but he still didn't trust them. He was quite myopic. If a
lens broke, he could never replace it. Sometimes he had a
nightmare in which his glasses dropped from his nose and
he reached for them and just missed and the glasses fell
down a mountainside, turning over and over in the air.

He pressed the glasses more firmly against his nose, walked
forward a few yards and examined the ground again. He
could detect two or three sets of footprints, maybe more.
From the look of the ground they had been made recently.

Miller found that he was beginning to tremble. He
squatted down beside the footprints and reminded himself

that he must not hope. The people who made those prints were probably dead.

Still, he had to make sure. He straightened up and began following the footprints. They led through a stubbled field to the edge of a forest. He stopped for a moment and listened.

It was a silent, beautiful September morning. The sun beat down on the barren fields, and light glinted from the stripped white branches of the forest. The only sounds he heard were the tired sigh of the wind and the background clicking of his geiger counter.

"Normal reading," Miller said to himself. "Whoever came this way must have had a geiger."

But they might not have used it properly. Perhaps they were contaminated, perhaps they were dying of radiation sickness. He couldn't allow himself to hope. He had stayed sane this long by not hoping, not wishing, not desiring.

"If they're dead," he told himself, "I'll give them decent burial." That thought exorcised the evil demons of hope and desire.

Within the forest, he lost the faint trail in the underbrush. He tried to continue in the same direction, but his geiger counter began to chatter furiously. He moved out at right angles, holding the geiger in front of him. When he had by-passed the hot spot he turned again, at an exact right angle, and walked parallel to the direction of the trail. Carefully he counted his paces. It wouldn't do for him to get caught in a pocket with radiation all around and no clear path out. That had happened to him three months ago, and the geiger's batteries had been nearly exhausted before he could find a way out. He had spare batteries in his knapsack now, but the danger was still there.

After about twenty yards he turned again to cross the trail, walking slowly, watching the ground.

He was lucky. He found the footprints again, and near them a fragment of cloth caught on a bramble bush. He plucked the cloth and put it in his pocket. The footprints looked very fresh. Did he dare allow himself a little hope?

No, not yet. He still remembered what had happened less than six months ago. He had climbed a small sandstone cliff to forage a warehouse on its top. At sunset he had come back down the cliff, and at the base he had found the body of a man. The man had been dead only a few hours. A submachine gun and a rifle were strapped to his shoulders, and his pockets were stuffed with grenades. They had been no protection against his subtlest enemy. The man had killed himself; the warm revolver was still in his hand.

Apparently he had been following Miller's footprints. When he had come to the base of the sandstone cliff, the footprints ended. Perhaps the man's stamina had been undermined by the harsh radiation burns across his chest and arms; perhaps the instant of shattered hope when the footprints ended in solid stone had been too much for him. Whatever the reason, he had blown out his brains at the foot of the cliff. Hope had killed him.

Miller had removed the man's armament and buried him. He thought about the weapons for the better part of a day. He was tempted to keep them. They might be very necessary in this shattered new world.

But finally he decided against keeping them. He was not going to violate the sternly held pledge of a lifetime; not after all he had seen. Besides, weapons at a time like this were too dangerous to the user. So he threw them into the nearest river.

That had been less than six months ago. Now it was Miller who followed footprints, through thin forest loam to a narrow stream of running water. When he had crossed it he was able to count, in the stiff mud, five separate sets of footprints. They were so recent that the water was still seeping into them. The people must have passed here within the half-hour.

He felt the demons of hope and desire stir within him. Surely it wouldn't be too unwise now to consider the possibility of meeting people? Yes, too unwise. The unleashed demons, once frustrated, turned against you, as they had turned against the man at the base of the sandstone cliff. Hope and desire were his most dangerous enemies. He didn't dare release the genies from the corked bottle deep in his mind.

He walked quickly along the trail, certain, from the increasing freshness of the prints, that he was moving faster than the presumed group of people. His geiger clucked contentedly to itself, satisfied with the low radiation level. The people ahead of him—if they were still alive—must be picking their way through with a geiger.

Survival had been so simple, really; but so few had managed it.

Miller had known the end was in sight when the Chinese

communists launched their large-scale amphibious assault against Formosa. At the beginning it had looked like a local war, as local as the angry little war being fought in Kuwait, and the U.N. police action on the Turkish-Bulgarian border.

But it was one war too many. Treaties, like chains, dragged country after country into the conflict. No nuclear weapons had been employed as yet, but their use was imminent.

Nugent Miller, associate professor of ancient history at Laurelville College in Tennessee, read the handwriting on the wall and began to set up caches of food in the Laurelville Caverns. He was thirty-eight at the time, and an ardent, lifelong pacifist. When the DEW line radar sent back word of unidentified missiles from the north, Miller was already packed and ready. He went at once to the Laurelville Caverns, one of whose mouths was less than a mile from the college. He was surprised when only fifty or so students and faculty joined him. Surely the warning was clear enough.

The bombs fell, and drove the group deeper into the labyrinth of caves and tunnels. After a week, the bombs stopped. The survivors started to the surface.

Miller checked the radiation at the cave mouth and found it lethal. They couldn't leave. Food had already run out, and radioactive debris was filtering down, forcing them deeper into the caverns.

By the fourth week, thirty-eight people had starved to death. The radiation at the entrances was still too high to permit leaving. Miller decided to go into the lower levels and try to locate a still-untouched food cache. Three others accompanied him. The rest decided to risk the radiation and break out.

Miller and his friends climbed deep into the darkness of the caverns. They were very weak, and not one of them was a trained speleologist. Two were killed in a rock fall. Miller and one man clung stubbornly to life. They couldn't locate the food cache; but they did find a stream of black water, and saw the luminous dots of fish in the water, blind fish who lived all their lives in the caves. They fished, and caught nothing. It was several days before Miller was able to block up a branch of the stream, trap several fish and land them. By then, his friend was dead.

Miller lived by the stream and worked out ways of catching fish. He kept time as best he could, and climbed painfully to the surface once a week to check the radiation. It took twelve weeks for it to drop enough to allow him to leave.

He never saw any of the others from the cave, although he did find a few of their bodies.

Outside, he tried to locate people, anywhere. But hard radiation had caught most of the survivors of the hydrogen bombings. Very few had been equipped with food stores or geiger counters. All, or nearly all, had gone out in search of food before the radiation had dropped to a tolerable level. Doubtless there were some survivors; but where, where?

For several months he had looked. Then he stopped looking. He assumed there were some people left in parts of Africa and Asia, in South America. He would never see them. Perhaps he would find a few on the North American continent some day. Perhaps not. In the meantime, he would go on living.

He lived, trekking south in the fall and returning north in the spring, a quiet man who had never wanted war, who hated killing with a passion that many had simulated but few had felt. He was a man who clung to many of his former habits as though the bombs had never fallen. He read books when he could find them, and apologetically collected paintings and sculptures, stealing them from the ghostly caretakers of the empty art galleries.

He was a man who, long before the Second World War, had promised himself never to kill a fellow human; and who now, after the Third World War, saw no reason to change that resolve. He was an amiable, boyish college type who had survived the death of the fittest and who, after the agonized destruction of a world, was still filled with high resolves and impeccable ideals. He was a man whom circumstance had forced to repress desire and abandon hope.

The footprints led through sparse underbrush, around a moss-covered granite boulder. He heard sounds.

"A gust of wind," he told himself.

He came around the boulder and stopped. In front of him, only a few yards away, were five people. To his starved eyes they looked like a crowd, an army, a multitude. They were camped around a small fire. It took him several seconds to assimilate this much information.

"Well I'll be damned," one of them said.

He adjusted. He took in the scene again. Five people, all of them women. Five women, dressed in ragged jeans and denim jackets, with rucksacks on the ground beside them, with crude spears propped up against the rucksacks.

"Who are you?" one of the women asked. She was the oldest, perhaps fifty years old. She was a short, stocky, strongly built woman with a square face and iron-gray hair, with strongly muscled arms and a brown, sinewy neck, with pince-nez—one lens cracked—perched incongruously on her large nose.

"Can't you talk?" the woman asked sharply.

"Yes, I can talk," Miller said. "Sorry. I was just surprised. You're the first women I've seen since the bombing."

"The first women?" she asked sharply. "Have you seen men?"

"Only dead ones," Miller said. He turned from her and looked at the other four. They were young, somewhere in their twenties, and Miller thought them inexpressibly beautiful. Undoubtedly they were different and distinct from each other; but to Miller, coming upon them as he would encounter an unknown race, they were alike in their alienness. Four comely animals, golden-skinned and long-limbed, with the great calm eyes of panthers.

"So you're the only man around," the older woman said. "Well, that won't constitute any problem."

The girls didn't speak. They were staring at him. Miller began to feel uncomfortable and self-conscious. He was considering the responsibilities of the situation, and the thoughts excited yet disturbed him.

"We might as well get introductions over with," the older woman said in her firm, matter-of-fact voice. "My name is Miss Denis."

Miller waited, but Miss Denis didn't introduce the girls. He said, "My name is Nugent Miller."

"Well, Mr. Miller, you're the first person we've encountered. Our story is really very simple. When I heard the alarms, I took the girls to the sub-basement of our school. The Charleton-Vaness School for Young Ladies, that is. I am—I was—an instructor in etiquette."

A colleague, Miller thought wryly.

"Naturally," Miss Denis went on, "I had equipped the shelter with supplies, as any prudent person should have done. But as few did. I had several geiger counters, in whose use I had familiarized myself. Some foolish people insisted upon leaving the shelter immediately after the bombs had stopped falling. I succeeded in impressing on these girls the dangers of radiation. It seeped down. We were forced to abandon the sub-basement and take refuge in the sewer system further down."

"We ate rats," one of the girls said.

"That's right, Suzie," Miss Denis said. "We ate rats and were very happy to get them. When the radiation subsided to a safe level, we came out. We have been doing nicely ever since."

The girls nodded in agreement. They were still watching Miller with their panther eyes. And Miller was watching them. He had fallen in love with all of them simultaneously and quite genuinely, particularly with Suzie because she had a name. But he hadn't fallen in love with the squat, strong-armed, matter-of-fact Miss Denis.

"My own experiences were quite similar," Miller said. "I went into the Laurelville Caverns. I didn't find any rats to eat, but I did consume some very odd-looking fish. I suppose the next thing is, what do we do?"

"Is it?" Miss Denis asked.

"I should think so. We survivors should stick together for mutual support and assistance. Shall we go to your camp or mine? I don't know how much foraging you've done. I've done quite a bit. Assembled a library and a few paintings, and a good stock of food."

"No," Miss Denis said.

"Well, if you insist upon your camp—"

"I do indeed. Our camp. And alone. That means without you, Mr. Miller."

Miller could hardly believe it. He looked at the girls. They looked back at him warily, their faces unreadable.

"Now listen," Miller said, "we need mutual support and assistance—"

"By which you mean the lasciviousness of the male," Miss Denis said.

"I didn't mean anything of the sort," Miller said. "If you insist upon talking about that now, I suppose we can just let nature take its course."

"Nature *has* taken its course," Miss Denis said. "It's only true course. We are five women. We have done very well together over the last months. Haven't we, girls?"

The girls nodded, but their eyes were still fixed upon Miller.

"We have no need," Miss Denis said, "of you or any other man. No need and no desire."

"I'm afraid I don't understand," Miller said, although he was beginning to.

"Men are responsible for all this," Miss Denis said. She waved her thick hand in an all-encompassing gesture. "Men ran the governments, men were the soldiers and the nuclear scientists, men started the war that has wiped out most of the human race. Even before the bombings I always warned my girls to beware of men. A lot of drivel was talked about equality of the sexes; in practice, woman was still man's chattel and his plaything. But when times were normal I couldn't explain my theories fully. The school would not have allowed it."

"I can understand that," Miller said.

"Now times are no longer normal. You men have messed things up once and for all, and you're not going to get another chance. Not if I have anything I can do about it."

"Maybe the girls don't feel that way," Miller said.

"I am educating the girls," Miss Denis said. "It's a slow process, but we have plenty of time. And I believe my lessons have begun to take hold. We've had a good time together, haven't we, girls?"

"Yes, Miss Denis," the girls chorused.

"And we don't need this man around the premises, do we?"

"No, Miss Denis."

"You see?"

"Now just a minute," Miller said. "I think you're laboring under a misapprehension. *Some* men have been responsible for wars. Not *all* men. I for example, was an ardent pacifist at a time when it was distinctly uncomfortable to be one. In the Second World War, I served in an ambulance unit. I have never taken a human life, and I never intend to."

"So you're a coward as well as a man," Miss Denis said.

"I do not consider myself a coward," Miller said. "I have been a conscientious objector out of conviction, not cowardice. My ambulance unit operated on the front lines, like soldiers, except that we were not armed. I have been under fire. I have been wounded, though not badly."

"How utterly heroic," Miss Denis said, and the girls laughed.

"I'm not trying to parade my accomplishments before you," Miller said. "I'm simply trying to make you see what sort of a man I am. Men differ, you know."

"They're all the same," Miss Denis said. "All of them.

Dirty, hairy, smelly, promiscuous beasts who start wars and kill women and children. Don't try to tell me about men."

"I must," Miller said. "You don't know much about them. Tell me, what did *you* do to stop the wars you hate so much?"

"What can any woman do?" Miss Denis asked. "The captives must follow the conquerers."

"Nonsense," Miller said. "There was plenty women could have done if they'd really wanted to stop wars. Have you ever read *Lysistrata*? Aristophanes tells how the women of Greece refused to cohabit with their husbands until they stopped fighting. It makes the point—"

"I have read the play," Miss Denis said. "It was hardly a practical solution."

"Why not? Wasn't it because too many of you women loved war and worshipped soldiers? You could have stopped it if you'd wanted to. But you didn't! Nietzsche said—"

"Don't stand there quoting your damned *men* authors at me," Miss Denis said. "Your logic is specious. The fact is, you men had the power and you abused it. You treated women as playthings, and you used the Earth as one big battleground until you warred yourselves right out of existence. You're finished now, washed up, over. You're an extinct species. You stand there with your funny hairy face and you look as strange as a dinosaur or an auk. Go off and die somewhere, Miller. We women are going to have our chance now."

"You may find breeding difficult," Miller said.

"But not impossible. I kept in very close touch with the latest work being done in parthenogenetic research. Reproduction without the male is distinctly possible."

"Perhaps it is," Miller said. "But you aren't a trained scientist. Even if you were, you don't have the equipment."

"But I do know the places where the research was carried out," Miss Denis said. "We may find one of the women scientists still alive. Our chance is even better of finding lab equipment intact. With that, plus my own knowledge of the subject, I think I can lick the problem."

"You'll never do it," Miller said.

"I think I will. But even if I can't, I'd rather see the race die out than let *men* take over again."

She was growing red-faced and angry. Miller said quietly, "I can well understand that you have grievances against men. *Some* men. But surely we can talk this through and reach some mutually satisfactory—"

"No! We've done all the talking we're going to do! Get out of here!"

"I'm not going," Miller said.

Miss Denis moved quickly to the pile of weapons and picked up a spear.

"Girls," she said, "get ready."

The girls were still fascinated with Miller. They hesitated a moment. Then, obedient to Miss Denis' strong personality, they took handfuls of rocks from their knapsacks. They were excited now. They watched Miss Denis expectantly.

"Are you leaving?" she asked.

"No!"

"Stone him!"

A hail of rocks flew through the air. Miller turned away to shield his geiger counter, and felt stones pelt him in the back and legs. He could hardly believe it was happening. These girls whom he loved—and especially Suzie—wouldn't be stoning him. They would stop in a moment, they would be ashamed.

But the rocks flew, and one caught him on the top of the head, half-stunning him. He shook his head, turned and ran forward, still holding the geiger counter. Miss Denis tried clumsily to impale him on her spear. He avoided the thrust and grabbed the spear with his left hand. They wrestled for it.

One-handed, he almost pulled it away; but Miss Denis, strong and squat as a bull, was too much for him. She wrenched the spear free and hit him over the head with the knobbed end. And the girls cheered!

Miller was on his knees now, and the rocks were still raining around him. A spear-point prodded him in the side. He rolled away from it and regained his footing.

"Kill him!" Miss Denis screamed. "Kill the dirty man!"

The girls, their faces flushed with excitement, advanced on him. Miller felt a spear graze his side. He turned and ran.

He didn't know how long he ran through the green twilight of the forest. At last he couldn't run any more. He drew his pocket knife and turned; but no one was following him.

Miller lay down on the cool ground and tried to think. That woman, that Miss Denis, must be crazy. An old man-hater, a hard-bitten Lesbian gone stark raving mad. And the girls? He was sure they hadn't wanted to hurt him.

Perhaps they loved him. But they were under the influence of the old bitch.

He checked and found that he hadn't lost his geiger counter or his glasses in the flight. He was grateful. Without them, it would be difficult to find his own camp.

He had always known that people were a little crazy. He should have realized that the survivors of an atomic holocaust would be even crazier than usual. That insane Miss Denis. Imagine *man* being an extinct species!

With a shock, Miller found that he could imagine it. After all, how many men had survived? How many women? What number of those survivors had geigers, what number would be able to overcome the hazards that lay ahead?

Still, that didn't affect him. The human race wasn't his responsibility. He had been a fool to release the demons of hope and desire. Now he would have to conquer them all over again. But he could do it. He would live the rest of his life among his books and paintings. Perhaps he would be the last truly civilized man.

Civilized . . . Miller shuddered and remembered the face of Suzie and the others, their panther eyes watching. Too bad he hadn't been able to effect some sort of compromise with Miss Denis. But under the circumstances there was nothing he could do—

Except abandon every principle he had ever lived by.

Could he do it? He looked at the knife in his hand and shuddered under the weight of the demons on his shoulders. His hand tightened around the hilt.

A moment later, the world's last civilized man was dead. With him perished the world's last pacifist and conscientious objector, the final art collector and ultimate bibliophile.

In the place of these admirable creatures was *Miller*, the small knife gripped in his hand, looking around the forest for something.

He found it. A lightning-blasted bough three feet long, and heavy.

Quickly he trimmed off the excess sprouts. Soon, Miss Denis was going to have the horried epitome of all hairy, smelly, dirty, club-wielding maledom bursting in upon her. He hoped she would have time to realize that she had called the beast to life herself. It would be quite a surprise for her.

And shortly after that, the girls were in for a surprise. Especially Suzie.

MEETING OF THE

MINDS

PART ONE

THE Quedak lay on a small hilltop and watched a slender jet of light descend through the sky. The feather-tailed jet was golden, and brighter than the sun. Poised above it was a glistening metallic object, fabricated rather than natural, hauntingly familiar. The Quedak tried to think what it was.

He couldn't remember. His memories had atrophied with his functions, leaving only scattered fragments of images. He searched among them now, leafing through his brief scraps of ruined cities, dying populations, a blue-water-filled canal, two moons, a spaceship . . .

That was it. The descending object was a *spaceship*. There had been many of them during the great days of the Quedak.

Those great days were over, buried forever beneath the powdery sands. Only the Quedak remained. He had life and he had a mission to perform. The driving urgency of his mission remained, even after memory and function had failed.

As the Quedak watched, the spaceship dipped lower. It wobbled and sidejets kicked out to straighten it. With a gentle explosion of dust, the spaceship settled tail first on the arid plain.

And the Quedak, driven by the imperative Quedak mission, dragged itself painfully down from the little hilltop.

Every movement was an agony. If he were a selfish creature, the Quedak would have died. But he was not selfish.
Quedaks owed a duty to the universe; and that spaceship,
after all the blank years, was a link to other worlds, to
planets where the Quedak could live again and give his
services to the native fauna.

He crawled, a centimeter at a time, and wondered whether
he had the strength to reach the alien spaceship before it
left this dusty, dead planet.

Captain Jensen of the spaceship *Southern Cross* was bored
sick with Mars. He and his men had been here for ten
days. They had found no important archeological specimens,
no tantalizing hints of ancient cities such as the *Polaris*
expedition had discovered at the South Pole. Here there was
nothing but sand, a few weary shrubs, and a rolling hill or
two. Their biggest find so far had been three pottery shards.

Jensen readjusted his oxygen booster. Over the rise of a
hill he saw his two men returning.

"Anything interesting?" he asked.

"Just this," said engineer Vayne, holding up an inch of
corroded blade without a handle.

"Better than nothing," Jensen said. "How about you,
Wilks?"

The navigator shrugged his shoulders. "Just photographs
of the landscape."

"OK," Jensen said. "Dump everything into the sterilizer
and let's get going."

Wilks looked mournful. "Captain, one quick sweep to the
north might turn up something really—"

"Not a chance," Jensen said. "Fuel, food, water, everything was calculated for a ten-day stay. That's three days
longer than *Polaris* had. We're taking off this evening."

The men nodded. They had no reason to complain. As
the second to land on Mars, they were sure of a small but
respectable footnote in the history books. They put their
equipment through the sterilizer vent, sealed it, and climbed
the ladder to the lock. Once they were inside, Vayne closed
and dogged the hatch, and started to open the inside pressure door.

"Hold it!" Jensen called out.

"What's the matter?"

"I thought I saw something on your boot," Jensen said.
"Something like a big bug."

Vayne quickly ran his hands down the sides of his boots. The two men circled him, examining his clothing.

"Shut that inner door," the captain said. "Wilks, did you see anything?"

"Not a thing," the navigator said. "Are you sure, Cap? We haven't found anything that looks like animal or insect life here. Only a few plants."

"I could have sworn I saw something," Jensen said. "Maybe I was wrong . . . Anyhow, we'll fumigate our clothes before we enter the ship proper. No sense taking any chance of bringing back some kind of Martian bug."

The men removed their clothing and boots and stuffed them into the chute. They searched the bare steel room carefully.

"Nothing here," Jensen said at last. "OK, let's go inside."

Once inside the ship, they sealed off the lock and fumigated it. The Quedak, who had crept inside earlier through the partially opened pressure door, listened to the distant hiss of gas. After a while he heard the jets begin to fire.

The Quedak retreated to the dark rear of the ship. He found a metal shelf and attached himself to the underside of it near the wall. After a while he felt the ship tremble.

The Quedak clung to the shelf during the long, slow flight through space. He had forgotten what spaceships were like, but now memory revived briefly. He felt blazing heat and freezing cold. Adjusting to the temperature changes drained his small store of vitality, and the Quedak began to wonder if he was going to die.

He *refused* to die. Not while there was still a possibility of accomplishing the Quedak mission.

In time he felt the harsh pull of gravity, and felt the main jets firing again. The ship was coming down to its planet.

After a routine landing, Captain Jensen and his men were taken to Medic Checkpoint, where they were thumped, probed and tested for any sign of disease.

Their spaceship was lowered to a flatcar and taken past rows of moonships and ICBMs to Decontamination Stage One. Here the sealed outer hull was washed down with powerful cleansing sprays. By evening, the ship was taken to Decontamination Stage Two.

A team of two inspectors equipped with bulky tanks and hoses undogged the hatch and entered, shutting the hatch behind them.

They began at the bow, methodically spraying as they moved toward the rear. Everything seemed in order; no animals or plants, no trace of mold such as the first Luna expedition had brought back.

"Do you really think this is necessary?" the assistant inspector asked. He had already requested a transfer to Flight Control.

"Sure it is," the senior inspector said. "Can't tell what these ships might bring in."

"I suppose so," the assistant said. "Still, a Martian whoosis wouldn't even be able to live on Earth. Would it?"

"How should I know?" the senior inspector said. "I'm no botanist. Maybe they don't know, either."

"Seems like a waste of—hey!"

"What is it?" the senior inspector asked.

"I thought I saw something," the assistant said. "Looked a little like a palmetto bug. Over by that shelf."

The senior inspector adjusted his respirator more snugly over his face and motioned to his assistant to do the same. He advanced slowly toward the shelf, unfastening a second nozzle from the pressure tank on his back. He turned it on, and a cloud of greenish gas sprayed out.

"There," the senior inspector said. "That should take care of your bug." He knelt down and looked under the shelf. "Nothing here."

"It was probably a shadow," the assistant said.

Together they sprayed the entire interior of the ship, paying particular attention to the small box of Martian artifacts. They left the gas-filled ship and dogged the hatch again.

"Now what?" the assistant asked.

"Now we leave the ship sealed for three days," the senior inspector said. "Then we inspect again. You find me the animal that'll live through that."

The Quedak, who had been clinging to the underside of the assistant's shoe between the heel and the sole, released his hold. He watched the shadowy biped figures move away, talking in their deep, rumbling, indecipherable voices. He felt tired and unutterably lonely.

But buoying him up was the thought of the Quedak mission. Only that was important. The first part of the mission was accomplished. He had landed safely on an inhabited planet. Now he needed food and drink. Then he had to have rest, a great deal of rest to restore his dormant faculties. After that he would be ready to give this world what it so obviously needed—the cooperation possible only through the Quedak mind.

He crept slowly down the shadowy yard, past the deserted hulls of spaceships. He came to a wire fence and sensed the high-voltage electricity running through it. Gauging his distance carefully, the Quedak jumped safely through one of the openings in the mesh.

This was a very different section. From here the Quedak could smell water and food. He moved hastily forward, then stopped.

He sensed the presence of a man. And something else. Something much more menacing.

"Who's there?" the watchman called out. He waited, his revolver in one hand, his flashlight in the other. Thieves had broken into the yards last week; they had stolen three cases of computer parts bound for Rio. Tonight he was ready for them.

He walked forward, an old, keen-eyed man holding his revolver in a rock-steady fist. The beam of his flashlight probed among the cargoes. The yellow light flickered along a great pile of precision machine tools for South Africa, past a water-extraction plant for Jordan and a pile of mixed goods for Rabaul.

"You better come out," the watchman shouted. His flashlight probed at sacks of rice for Shanghai and power saws for Burma. Then the beam of light stopped abruptly.

"I'll be damned," the watchman said. Then he laughed. A huge and red-eyed rat was glaring into the beam of his flashlight. It had something in its jaws, something that looked like an unusually large cockroach.

"Good eating," the watchman said. He holstered his revolver and continued his patrol.

A large black animal had seized the Quedak, and he felt heavy jaws close over his back. He tried to fight; but, blinded by a sudden beam of yellow light, he was betrayed by total and enervating confusion.

The yellow light went off. The black beast bit down hard on the Quedak's armored back. The Quedak mustered his remaining strength, and, uncoiling his long, scorpion-jointed tail, lashed out.

He missed, but the black beast released him hastily. They circled each other, the Quedak hoisting his tail for a second blow, the beast unwilling to turn loose this prey.

The Quedak waited for his chance. Elation filled him. This pugnacious animal could be the first, the first on this planet to experience the Quedak mission. From this humble creature a start could be made. . . .

The beast sprang and its white teeth clicked together viciously. The Quedak moved out of the way and its barb-headed tail flashed out, fastening itself in the beast's back. The Quedak held on grimly while the beast leaped and squirmed. Setting his feet, the Quedak concentrated on the all-important task of pumping a tiny white crystal down the length of his tail and under the beast's skin.

But this most important of the Quedak faculties was still dormant. Unable to accomplish anything, the Quedak released his barbs, and, taking careful aim, accurately drove his sting home between the black beast's eyes. The blow, as the Quedak had known, was lethal.

The Quedak took nourishment from the body of its dead foe; regretfully, for by inclination the Quedak was herbivorous. When he had finished, the Quedak knew that he was in desperate need of a long period of rest. Only after that could the full Quedak powers be regained.

He crawled up and down the piles of goods in the yard, looking for a place to hide. Carefully he examined several bales. At last he reached a stack of heavy boxes. One of the boxes had a crack just large enough to admit him.

The Quedak crawled inside, down the shiny, oil-slick surface of a machine, to the far end of the box. There he went into the dreamless, defenseless sleep of the Quedak, serenely trusting in what the future would bring.

PART TWO

I

The big gaff-headed schooner was pointed directly at the reef-enclosed island, moving toward it with the solidity of an express train. The sails billowed under powerful gusts of the northwest breeze, and the rusty Allison-Chambers diesel rumbled beneath a teak grating. The skipper and mate stood on the bridge deck and watched the reef approach.

"Anything yet?" the skipper asked. He was a stocky, bald-

ing man with a perpetual frown on his face. He had been sailing his schooner among the uncharted shoals and reefs of the
Southwest Pacific for twenty-five years. He frowned because
his old ship was not insurable. His deck cargo, however, *was*
insured. Some of it had come all the way from Ogdensville,
that transshipment center in the desert where spaceships
landed.

"Not a thing," the mate said. He was watching the dazzling
white wall of coral, looking for the gleam of blue that would
reveal the narrow pass to the inner lagoon. This was his
first trip to the Solomon Islands. A former television repairman in Sydney before he got the wanderlust, the mate wondered if the skipper had gone crazy and planned a spectacular
suicide against the reef.

"Still nothing!" he shouted. "Shoals ahead!"

"I'll take it," the skipper said to the helmsman. He gripped
the wheel and watched the unbroken face on the reef.

"Nothing," the mate said. "Skipper, we'd better come
about."

"Not if we're going to get through the pass," the skipper
said. He was beginning to get worried. But he had promised
to deliver goods to the American treasure-hunters on this
island, and the skipper's word was his bond. He had picked
up the cargo in Rabaul and made his usual stops at the
settlements on New Georgia and Malaita. When he finished
here, he could look forward to a thousand-mile run to New
Caledonia.

"There it is!" the mate shouted.

A thin slit of blue had appeared in the coral wall. They
were less than thirty yards from it now, and the old schooner
was making close to eight knots.

As the ship entered the pass, the skipper threw the wheel
hard over. The schooner spun on its keel. Coral flashed by
on either side, close enough to touch. There was a metallic
shriek as an upper mainmast spreader snagged and came
free. Then they were in the pass, bucking a six-knot current.

The mate pushed the diesel to full throttle, then sprang
back to help the skipper wrestle with the wheel. Under sail
and power the schooner forged through the pass, scraped by
an outcropping to port, and came onto the placid surface
of the lagoon.

The skipper mopped his forehead with a large blue ban-
danna. "Very snug work," he said.

"Snug!" the mate cried. He turned away, and the skipper smiled a brief smile.

They slid past a small ketch riding at anchor. The native hands took down sail and the schooner nosed up to a rickety pier that jutted out from the beach. Lines were made fast to palm trees. From the fringe of jungle above the beach a white man came down, walking briskly in the noonday heat.

He was very tall and thin, with knobby knees and elbows. The fierce Melanesian sun had burned out but not tanned him, and his nose and cheekbones were peeling. His horn-rimmed glasses had broken at the hinge and been repaired with a piece of tape. He looked eager, boyish, and curiously naive.

One hell-of-a-looking treasure-hunter, the mate thought.

"Glad to see you!" the man called out. "We'd about given you up for lost."

"Not likely," the skipper said. "Mr. Sorensen, I'd like you to meet my new mate, Mr. Willis."

"Glad to meet you, Professor," the mate said.

"I'm not a professor," Sorensen said, "but thanks anyhow."

"Where are the others?" the skipper asked.

"Out in the jungle," Sorensen said. "All except Drake, and he'll be down here shortly. You'll stay a while, won't you?"

"Only to unload," the skipper said. "Have to catch the tide out of here. How's the treasure-hunting?"

"We've done a lot of digging," Sorensen said. "We still have our hopes."

"But no doubloons yet?" the skipper asked. "No pieces of eight?"

"Not a damned one," Sorensen said wearily. "Did you bring the newspapers, Skipper?"

"That I did," Sorenson replied. "They're in the cabin. Did you hear about that second spaceship going to Mars?"

"Heard about it on the short wave," Sorensen said. "It didn't bring back much, did it?"

"Practically nothing. Still, just think of it. *Two* spaceships to Mars, and I hear they're getting ready to put one on Venus."

The three men looked around them and grinned.

"Well," the skipper said, "I guess maybe the space age hasn't reached the Southwest Pacific yet. And it certainly hasn't gotten to *this* place. Come on, let's unload the cargo."

This place was the island of Vuanu, southernmost of the Solomons, almost in the Louisade Archipelago. It was a fair-sized volcanic island, almost twenty miles long and several wide. Once it had supported half a dozen native villages. But the population had begun to decline after the depredations of the blackbirders in the 1850s. Then a measles epidemic wiped out almost all the rest, and the survivors emigrated to New Georgia. A ship-watcher had been stationed here during the Second World War, but no ships had come this way. The Japanese invasion had poured across New Guinea and the upper Solomons, and further north through Micronesia. At the end of the war Vuanu was still deserted. It was not made into a bird sanctuary like Canton Island, or a cable station like Christmas Island, or a refueling point like Cocos-Keeling. No one even wanted to explode alphabet bombs on it. Vuanu was a worthless, humid, jungle-covered piece of land, free to anyone who wanted it.

William Sorensen, general manager of a chain of liquor stores in California, decided he wanted it.

Sorensen's hobby was treasure-hunting. He had looked for Lafitte's treasure in Louisiana and Texas, and for the Lost Dutchman Mine in Arizona. He had found neither. His luck had been better on the wreck-strewn Gulf coast, and on an expedition to Dagger Cay in the Caribbean he had found a double handful of Spanish coins in a rotting canvas bag. The coins were worth about three thousand dollars. The expedition had cost very much more, but Sorensen felt amply repaid.

For many years he had been interested in the Spanish treasure galleon *Santa Teresa*. Contemporary accounts told how the ship, heavily laden with bullion, sailed from Manila in 1689. The clumsy ship, caught in a storm, had run off to the south and been wrecked. Eighteen survivors managed to get ashore with the treasure. They buried it, and set sail for the Philippines in the ship's pinnace. Two of them were alive when the boat reached Manila.

The treasure island was tentatively identified as one of the Solomons. But which one?

No one knew. Treasure-hunters looked for the cache on Bougainville and Buka. There was a rumor about it on Malaita, and even Ontong Java received an expedition. But no treasure was recovered.

Sorensen, researching the problem thoroughly, decided that the *Santa Teresa* had sailed completely through the Solomons, almost to the Louisades. The ship must have escaped destruction until it crashed into the reef at Vuanu.

His desire to search for the treasure might have remained

only a dream if he hadn't met Dan Drake. Drake was also an amateur treasure-hunter. More important, he owned a fifty-five-foot Hanna ketch.

Over an evening's drinks the Vuanu expedition was born. Additional members were recruited. Drake's ketch was put into seagoing condition, equipment and money saved or gathered. Several other possible treasure sites in the Southwest Pacific were researched. Finally, vacation time was synchronized and the expedition got under way.

They had put in three months' work on Vuanu already. Their morale was high, in spite of inevitable conflicts between members. This schooner, bringing in supplies from Sydney and Rabaul, was the last civilized contact they would have for another six months.

While Sorensen nervously supervised, the crew of the schooner unloaded the cargo. He didn't want any of the equipment, some of it shipped over six thousand miles, to be broken now. No replacements were possible; whatever they didn't have, they would have to do without. He breathed out in relief when the last crate, containing a metals detector, was safely hoisted over the side and put on the beach above the high-water mark.

There was something odd about that box. He examined it and found a quarter-sized hole in one end. It had not been properly sealed.

Dan Drake, the co-manager of the expedition, joined him. "What's wrong?" Drake asked.

"Hole in that crate," Sorensen said. "Salt water might have gotten in. We'll be in tough shape if this detector doesn't work."

Drake nodded. "We better open it and see." He was a short, deeply tanned, broad-chested man with close-cropped black hair and a straggly mustache. He wore an old yachting cap jammed down over his eyes, giving his face a tough bulldog look. He pulled a big screwdriver from his belt and inserted it into the crack.

"Wait a moment," Sorensen said. "Let's get it up to the camp first. Easier to carry the crate than something packed in grease."

"Right," Drake said. "Take the other end."

The camp was built in a clearing a hundred yards from the beach, on the site of an abandoned native village. They had been able to rethatch several huts, and there was an old copra shed with a galvanized iron roof where they stored their supplies. Here they got the benefit of any breeze from the sea. Beyond the clearing, the gray-green jungle sprang up like a solid wall.

Sorensen and Drake set the case down. The skipper, who had accompanied them with the newspapers, looked around at the bleak huts and shook his head.

"Would you like a drink, Skipper?" Sorensen asked. "Afraid we can't offer any ice."

"A drink would be fine," the skipper said. He wondered what drove men to a godforsaken place like this in search of imaginary Spanish treasure.

Sorensen went into one of the huts and brought out a bottle of Scotch and a tin cup. Drake had taken out his screwdriver and was vigorously ripping boards off the crate.

"How does it look?" Sorensen asked.

"It's OK," Drake said, gently lifting out the metals detector. "Heavily greased. Doesn't seem like there was any damage—"

He jumped back. The skipper had come forward and stamped down heavily on the sand.

"What's the matter?" Sorensen asked.

"Looked like a scorpion," the skipper said. "Damned thing crawled right out of your crate there. Might have bit you."

Sorensen shrugged. He had gotten used to the presence of an infinite number of insects during his three months on Vuanu. Another bug more or less didn't seem to make much difference.

"Another drink?" he asked.

"Can't do it," the skipper said regretfully. "I'd better get started. All your party healthy?"

"All healthy so far," Sorensen said. He smiled. "Except for some bad cases of gold fever."

"You'll never find gold in this place," the skipper said seriously. "I'll look in on you in about six months. Good luck."

After shaking hands, the skipper went down to the beach and boarded his ship. As the first pink flush of sunset touched the sky, the schooner was under way. Sorensen and Drake watched it negotiate the pass. For a few minutes its masts were visible above the reef. Then they had dipped below the horizon.

"That's that," Drake said. "Us crazy American treasure-hunters are alone again."

"You don't think he suspected anything?" Sorensen asked.

"Definitely not. As far as he's concerned, we're just crack-pots."

Grinning, they looked back at their camp. Under the copra shed was nearly fifty thousand dollars worth of gold and silver bullion, dug out of the jungle and carefully reburied. They had located a part of the *Santa Teresa* treasure during their first month on the island. There was every indication of more to come. Since they had no legal title to the land, the expedition was not eager to let the news get out. Once it was known, every gold-hungry vagabond from Perth to Papeete would be heading to Vuanu.

"The boys'll be in soon," Drake said. "Let's get some stew going."

"Right," Sorensen said. He took a few steps and stopped. "That's funny."

"What is?"

"That scorpion the skipper squashed. It's gone."

"Maybe he missed it," Drake said. "Or maybe he just pushed it down into the sand. What difference does it make?"

"None, I guess," Sorensen said.

II

Edward Eakins walked through the jungle with a long-handled spade on his shoulder, sucking reflectively on a piece of candy. It was the first he'd had in weeks, and he was enjoying it to the utmost. He was in very good spirits. The schooner yesterday had brought in not only machinery and replacement parts, but also candy, cigarettes and food. He had eaten scrambled eggs this morning, and real bacon. The expedition was becoming almost civilized.

Something rustled in the bushes near him. He marched on, ignoring it.

He was a lean, sandy-haired man, amiable and slouching, with pale blue eyes and an unprepossessing manner. He felt very lucky to have been taken on the expedition. His gas station didn't put him on a financial par with the others, and he hadn't been able to put up a full share of the money. He still felt guilty about that. He had been accepted because he was an eager and indefatigable treasure-hunter with a good knowledge of jungle ways. Equally important, he was a skilled radio operator and repairman. He had kept the transmitter on the ketch in working condition in spite of salt water and mildew.

He could pay his full share now, of course. But *now*, when they were practically rich, didn't really count. He wished there were some way he could—

There was that rustle in the bushes again.

Eakins stopped and waited. The bushes trembled. And out stepped a mouse.

Eakins was amazed. The mice on this island, like most wild animal life, were terrified of man. Although they feasted off the refuse of the camp—when the rats didn't get it first— they carefully avoided any contact with humans.

"You better get yourself home," Eakins said to the mouse.

The mouse stared at him. He stared back. It was a pretty little mouse, no more than four or five inches long, and colored a light tawny brown. It didn't seem afraid.

"So long, mouse," Eakins said. "I got work to do." He shifted his spade to the other shoulder and turned to go. As he turned, he caught a flash of brown out of the corner of his eye. Instinctively he ducked. The mouse whirled past him, turned, and gathered itself for another leap.

"Mouse, are you out of your head?" Eakins asked.

The mouse bared its tiny teeth and sprang. Eakins knocked it aside.

"Now get the hell out of here," he said. He was beginning to wonder if the rodent was crazy. Did it have rabies, per- haps?

The mouse gathered itself for another charge. Eakins lifted the spade off his shoulders and waited. When the mouse sprang, he met it with a carefully timed blow. Then carefully, regretfully, he battered it to death.

"Can't have rabid mice running around," he said.

But the mouse hadn't seemed rabid; it had just seemed very determined.

Eakins scratched his head. Now what, he wondered, had gotten into that little mouse?

In the camp that evening, Eakins' story was greeted with hoots of laughter. It was just like Eakins to be attacked by a mouse. Several men suggested that he go armed in case the mouse's family wanted revenge. Eakins just smiled sheep- ishly.

Two days later, Sorensen and Al Cable were finishing up a morning's hard work at Site 4, two miles from the camp. The metals detector had shown marked activity at this spot.

They were seven feet down and nothing had been produced yet except a high mound of yellow-brown earth.

"That detector must be wrong," Cable said, wiping his face wearily. He was a big, pinkish man. He had sweated off twenty pounds on Vuanu, picked up a bad case of prickly heat, and had enough treasure-hunting to last him a lifetime. He wished he were back in Baltimore taking care of his used-car agency. He didn't hesitate to say so, often and loudly. He was one member who had not worked out well.

"Nothing wrong with the detector," Sorensen said. "Trouble is, we're digging in swampy ground. The cache must have sunk."

"It's probably a hundred feet down," Cable said, stabbing angrily at the gluey mud.

"Nope," Sorensen said. "There's volcanic rock under us, no more than twenty feet down."

"Twenty feet? We should have a bulldozer."

"Might be costly bringing one in," Sorensen said mildly. "Come on, Al, let's get back to camp."

Sorensen helped Cable out of the excavation. They cleared off their tools and started toward the narrow path leading back to the camp. They stopped abruptly.

A large, ugly bird had stepped out of the brush. It was standing on the path, blocking their way.

"What in hell is that?" Cable asked.

"A cassowary," Sorensen said.

"Well, let's boot it out of the way and get-going."

"Take it easy," Sorensen said. "If anyone does any booting, it'll be the bird. Back away slowly."

The cassowary was nearly five feet high, a black-feathered ostrichlike bird standing erect on powerful legs. Each of its feet was three-toed, and the toes curved into heavy talons. It had a yellowish, bony head and short, useless wings. From its neck hung a brilliant wattle colored red, green, and purple.

"Is it dangerous?" Cable asked.

Sorensen nodded. "Natives on New Guinea have been kicked to death by those birds."

"Why haven't we seen it before?" Cable asked.

"They're usually very shy," Sorensen said. "They stay as far from people as they can."

"This one sure isn't shy," Cable said, as the cassowary took a step toward them. "Can we run?"

"The bird can run a lot faster," Sorensen said. "I don't suppose you have a gun with you?"

"Of course not. There's been nothing to shoot."

Backing away, they held their spades like spears. The brush crackled and an anteater emerged. It was followed by a wild pig. The three beasts converged on the men, backing them toward the dense wall of the jungle.

"They're herding us," Cable said, his voice going shrill.

"Take it easy," Sorensen said. "The cassowary is the only one we have to watch out for."

"Aren't anteaters dangerous?"

"Only to ants."

"The hell you say," Cable said. "Bill, the animals on this island have gone crazy. Remember Eakins' mouse?"

"I remember it," Sorensen said. They had reached the far edge of the clearing. The beasts were in front of them, still advancing, with the cassowary in the center. Behind them lay the jungle—and whatever they were being herded toward.

"We'll have to make a break for it," Sorensen said.

"That damned bird is blocking the trail."

"We'll have to knock him over," Sorensen said. "Watch out for his feet. Let's go!"

They raced toward the cassowary, swinging their spades. The cassowary hesitated, unable to make up its mind between targets. Then it turned toward Cable and its right leg lashed out. The partially deflected blow sounded like the flat of a meat cleaver against a side of beef. Cable grunted and collapsed, clutching his ribs.

Sorensen stabbed, and the honed edge of his spade nearly severed the cassowary's head from its body. The wild pig and the anteater were coming at him now. He flailed with his spade, driving them back. Then, with a strength he hadn't known he possessed, he stooped, lifted Cable across his shoulders and ran down the path.

A quarter of a mile down he had to stop, completely out of breath. There were no sounds behind him. The other animals were apparently not following. He went back to the wounded man.

Cable had begun to recover consciousness. He was able to walk, half-supported by Sorensen. When they reached the camp, Sorensen called everybody in for a meeting. He counted heads while Eakins taped up Cable's side. Only one man was missing.

"Where's Drake?" Sorensen asked.

"He's across the island at North Beach, fishing," said Tom Recetich. "Want me to get him?"

Sorensen hesitated. Finally he said, "No. I'd better explain what we're up against. Then we'll issue the guns. *Then* we'll try to find Drake."

"Man, what's going on?" Recetich asked.

Sorensen began to explain what had happened at Site 4.

Fishing provided an important part of the expedition's food and there was no work Drake liked better. At first he had gone out with face mask and spear gun. But the sharks in this corner of the world were numerous, hungry and aggressive. So, regretfully, he had given up skin diving and set out handlines on the leeward side of the island.

The lines were out now, and Drake lay in the shade of a palm tree, half asleep, his big forearms folded over his chest. His dog, Oro, was prowling the beach in search of hermit crabs. Oro was a good-natured mutt, part Airedale, part terrier, part unknown. He was growling at something now.

"Leave the crabs alone," Drake called out. "You'll just get nipped again."

Oro was still growling. Drake rolled over and saw that the dog was standing stiff-legged over a large insect. It looked like some kind of scorpion.

"Oro, leave that blasted—"

Before Drake could move, the insect sprang. It landed on Oro's neck and the jointed tail whipped out. Oro yelped once. Drake was on his feet instantly. He swatted at the bug, but it jumped off the dog's neck and scuttled into the brush.

"Take it easy, old boy," Drake said. "That's a nasty-looking wound. Might be poisoned. I better open it up."

He held the panting dog firmly and drew his boat knife. He had operated on the dog for snake bite in Central America, and in the Adirondacks he had held him down and pulled porcupine quills out of his mouth with a pair of pliers. The dog always knew he was being helped. He never struggled.

This time, the dog bit.

"Oro!" Drake grabbed the dog at the jaw hinge with his free hand. He brought pressure to bear, paralyzing the muscles, forcing the dog's jaws open. He pulled his hand out and flung the dog away. Oro rolled to his feet and advanced on him again.

"Stand!" Drake shouted. The dog kept coming, edging around to get between the ocean and the man.

Turning, Drake saw the bug emerge from the jungle and creep toward him. His dog had circled around and was trying to drive him toward the bug.

Drake didn't know what was going on, and he decided he'd better not stay to find out. He picked up his knife and threw it at the bug. He missed. The bug was almost within jumping distance.

Drake ran toward the ocean. When Oro tried to intercept him, he kicked the dog out of the way and plunged into the water.

He began to swim around the island to the camp, hoping he'd make it before the sharks got him.

III

At the camp, rifles and revolvers were hastily wiped clean of cosmoline and passed around. Binoculars were taken out and adjusted. Cartridges were divided up, and the supply of knives, machetes and hatchets quickly disappeared. The expedition's two walkie-talkies were unpacked, and the men prepared to move out in search of Drake. Then they saw him, swimming vigorously around the edge of the island.

He waded ashore, tired but uninjured. He and the others put their information together and reached some unhappy conclusions.

"Do you mean to say," Cable demanded, "that a *bug* is doing all this?"

"It looks that way," Sorensen said. "We have to assume that it's able to exercise some kind of thought control. Maybe hypnotic or telepathic."

"It has to sting first," Drake said. "That's what it did with Oro."

"I just can't imagine a scorpion doing all that," Recetich said.

"It's not a scorpion," Drake said. "I saw it close up. It's got a tail like a scorpion, but its head is damn near four times as big, and its body is different. Up close, it doesn't look like anything you ever saw before."

"Do you think it's native to this island?" asked Monty Byrnes, a treasure-seeker from Indianapolis.

"I doubt it," Drake said. "If it is, why did it leave us and the animals alone for three months?"

"That's right," Sorensen said. "All our troubles began just after the schooner came. The schooner must have brought it from somewhere. . . . Hey!"

"What is it?" Drake asked.

"Remember that scorpion the skipper tried to squash? It came out of the detector crate. Do you think it could be the same one?"

Drake shrugged his shoulders. "Could be. Seems to me our problem right now isn't finding out where it came from. We have to figure out what to do about it."

"If it can control animals," Byrnes said, "I wonder if it can control men."

They were all silent. They had moved into a circle near the copra shed, and while they talked they watched the jungle for any sign of insect or animal life.

Sorensen said, "We'd better radio for help."

"If we do that," Recetich said, "somebody's going to find out about the *Santa Teresa* treasure. We'll be overrun in no time."

"Maybe so," Sorensen said. "But at the worst, we've cleared expenses. We've even made a small profit."

"And if we don't get help," Drake said, "we may be in no condition to take anything out of here."

"The problem isn't as bad as all that," Byrnes said. "We've got guns. We can take care of the animals."

"You haven't seen the bug yet," Drake said.

"We'll squash it."

"That won't be easy," Drake said. "It's faster than hell. And how are you going to squash it if it comes into your hut some night while you're asleep? We could post guards and they wouldn't even see the thing."

Byrnes shuddered involuntarily. "Yeah, I guess you're right. Maybe we'd better radio for help."

Eakins stood up. "Well, gents," he said, "I guess that means me. I just hope the batteries on the ketch are up to charge."

"It'll be dangerous going out there," Drake said. "We'll draw lots."

Eakins was amused. "We will? How many of you can operate a transmitter?"

Drake said, "I can."

"No offense meant," Eakins said, "but you don't operate

that set of yours worth a damn. You don't even know Morse for key transmission. And can you fix the set if it goes out?"

"No," Drake said. "But the whole thing is too risky. We all should go."

Eakins shook his head. "Safest thing all around is if you cover me from the beach. That bug probably hasn't thought about the ketch yet."

Eakins stuck a tool kit in his pocket and strapped one of the camp's walkie-talkies over his shoulder. He handed the other one to Sorensen. He hurried down the beach past the launch and pushed the small dinghy into the water. The men of the expedition spread out, their rifles ready. Eakins got into the dinghy and started rowing across the quiet lagoon.

They saw him tie up to the ketch and pause a moment, looking around. Then he climbed aboard. Quickly he slid back the hatch and went inside.

"Everything all right?" Sorensen asked.

"No touble yet," Eakins said, his voice sounding thin and sharp over the walkie-talkie. "I'm at the transmitter now, turning it on. It needs a couple of minutes to warm up."

Drake nudged Sorensen. "Look over there."

On the reef, almost hidden by the ketch, something was moving. Using binoculars, Sorensen could see three big gray rats slipping into the water. They began swimming toward the ketch.

"Start firing!" Sorensen said. "Eakins, get out of there!"

"I've got the transmitter going," Eakins said. "I just need a couple of minutes more to get a message off."

Bullets sent up white splashes around the swimming rats. One was hit; the other two managed to put the ketch between them and the riflemen. Studying the reef with his binoculars, Sorensen saw an anteater cross the reef and splash into the water. It was followed by a wild pig.

There was a crackle of static from the walkie-talkie. Sorensen called, "Eakins, have you got that message off?"

"Haven't sent it," Eakins called back. "Listen, Bill. We *mustn't* send any messages! That bug wants—" He stopped abruptly.

"What is it?" Sorensen asked. "What's happening?"

Eakins had appeared on deck, still holding the walkie-talkie. He was backing toward the stern.

"Hermit crabs," he said. "They climbed up the anchor line. I'm going to swim to shore."

"Don't do it," Sorensen said.

"Gotta do it," Eakins said. "They'll probably follow me. All of you come out here and *get that transmitter*. Bring it ashore."

Through his binoculars, Sorensen could see a solid gray carpet of hermit crabs crawling down the deck and waterways of the ketch. Eakins jumped into the water. He swam furiously toward shore, and Sorensen saw the rats turn and follow him. Hermit crabs swarmed off the boat, and the wild pig and the anteater paddled after him, trying to head him off before he reached the beach.

"Come on," Sorensen said. "I don't know what Eakins figured out, but we better get that transmitter while we have a chance."

They ran down the beach and put the launch into the water. Two hundred yards away, Eakins had reached the far edge of the beach with the animals in close pursuit. He broke into the jungle, still clinging to his walkie-talkie.

"Eakins?" Sorensen asked into the walkie-talkie.

"I'm all right," Eakins said, panting hard for air. "Get that transmitter, and don't forget the batteries!"

The men boarded the ketch. Working furiously, they ripped the transmitter off its bulkhead and dragged it up the companionway steps. Drake came last, carrying a twelve-volt battery. He went down again and brought up a second battery. He hesitated a moment, then went below for a third time.

"Drake!" Sorensen shouted. "Quit holding us up!"

Drake reappeared, carrying the ketch's two radio direction finders and the compass. He handed them down and jumped into the launch.

"OK," he said. "Let's go."

They rowed to the beach. Sorensen was trying to re-establish contact with Eakins on the walkie-talkie, but all he could hear was static. Then, as the launch grounded on the beach, he heard Eakins' voice.

"I'm surrounded," he said, very quietly. "I guess I'll have to see what Mr. Bug wants. Maybe I can swat him first, though."

There was a long silence. Then Eakins said, "It's coming toward me now. Drake was right. It sure isn't like any bug *I've* ever seen. I'm going to swat hell out of—"

They heard him scream, more in surprise than pain.

Sorensen said, "Eakins, can you hear me? Where are you? Can we help?"

"It sure *is* fast," Eakins said, his voice conversational again. "Fastest damned bug I've ever seen. Jumped on my neck, stung me and jumped off again."

"How do you feel?" Sorensen asked.

"Fine," Eakins said. "Hardly felt the sting."

"Where is the bug now?"

"Back in the bush."

"The animals?"

"They went away. You know," Eakins said, "maybe this thing doesn't work on humans. Maybe—"

"What?" Sorensen asked. "What's happening now?"

There was a long silence. Then Eakins' voice, low-pitched and calm, came over the walkie-talkie.

"We'll speak with you again later," Eakins said. "We must take consultation now and decide what to do with you."

"Eakins!"

There was no answer from the other end of the walkie-talkie.

IV

Returning to their camp, the men were in a mood of thorough depression. They couldn't understand what had happened to Eakins and they didn't feel like speculating on it. The ravaging afternoon sun beat down, reflecting heat back from the white sand. The damp jungle steamed, and appeared to creep toward them like a huge and sleepy green dragon, trapping them against the indifferent sea. Gun barrels grew too hot to touch, and the water in the canteens was as warm as blood. Overhead, thick gray cumulus clouds began to pile up; it was the beginning of the monsoon season.

Drake sat in the shade of the copra shed. He shook off his lethargy long enough to inspect the camp from the viewpoint of defense. He saw the encircling jungle as enemy territory. In front of it was an area fifty yards deep which they had cleared. This no man's land could perhaps be defended for a while.

Then came the huts and the copra shed, their last line of defense, leading to the beach and the sea.

The expedition had been in complete control of this island for better than three months. Now they were pinned to a small and precarious beachhead.

Drake glanced at the lagoon behind him and remembered that there was still one line of retreat open. If the bug and his damned menagerie pressed too hard, they could still escape in the ketch. With luck.

Sorensen came over and sat down beside him. "What are you doing?" he asked.

Drake grinned sourly. "Planning our master strategy."

"How does it look?"

"I think we can hold out," Drake said. "We've got plenty of ammo. If necessary, we'll interdict the cleared area with gasoline. We certainly aren't going to let that bug push us off the island." He thought for a moment. "But it's going to be damned hard digging for treasure."

Sorensen nodded. "I wonder what the bug wants."

"Maybe we'll find out from Eakins," Drake said.

They had to wait half an hour. Then Eakins' voice came, sharp and shrill over the walkie-talkie.

"Sorensen? Drake?"

"We're here," Drake said. "What did that damned bug do to you?"

"Nothing," Eakins said. "You are talking to that bug now. My name is the Quedak."

"My God," Drake said to Sorensen, "that bug must have hypnotized him!"

"No. You are not speaking to a hypnotized Eakins. Nor are you speaking to a creature who is simply using Eakins as a mouthpiece. Nor are you speaking to the Eakins who was. You are speaking to many individuals who are one."

"I don't get that," Drake said.

"It's very simple," Eakins' voice replied. "I am the Quedak, the totality. But my totality is made up of separate parts, which are Eakins, several rats, a dog named Oro, a pig, an anteater, a cassowary—"

"Hold on," Sorensen said. "Let me get this straight. This is *not* Eakins I'm speaking to. This is the—the Quedak?"

"That is correct."

"And you control Eakins and the others? You speak through Eakins' mouth?"

"Also correct. But that doesn't mean that the personalities of the others are obliterated. Quite the contrary, the Quedak state is a federation in which the various member parts retain their idiosyncrasies, their individual needs and desires. They give their knowledge, their power, their special outlook to the Quedak whole. The Quedak is the coordinating and command center; but the individual parts supply the knowledge, the insights, the special skills. And together we form the Great Cooperation."

"Cooperation?" Drake said. "But you did all this by force!"

"It was necessary in the beginning. Otherwise, how would other creatures have known about the Great Cooperation?"

"Would they stay if you released your control over them?" Drake asked.

"That is a meaningless question. We form a single indivisible entity now. Would your arm return to you if you cut if off?"

"It isn't the same thing."

"It is," Eakins' voice said. "We are a single organism. We are still growing. And we welcome you wholeheartedly into the Great Cooperation."

"To hell with that," Drake said.

"But you must join," the Quedak told them. "It is the Quedak Mission to coordinate all sentient creatures into a single collective organism. Believe me, there is only the most trifling loss of the individuality you prize so highly. And you gain so much more! You learn the viewpoints and special knowledge of all other creatures. Within the Quedak framework you can fully realize your potentialities—"

"No!"

"I am sorry," the Quedak said. "The Quedak Mission must be fulfilled. You will not join us willingly?"

"Never," Drake said.

"Then *we* will join *you*," the Quedak said.

There was a click as he turned off the walkie-talkie.

From the fringe of the jungle, several rats appeared. They hesitated, just out of rifle range. A bird of paradise flew overhead, hovering over the cleared area like an observation plane. As the men watched, the rats began to run forward in long zigzags.

"Start firing," Drake called out. "But go easy with the ammo."

The men began to fire. But it was difficult to sight on the quick-moving rats against the grayish-brown clearing. And almost immediately, the rats were joined by a dozen hermit crabs. They had an uncanny knack for moving when no one was watching them, darting forward, then freezing against the neutral background.

They saw Eakins appear on the fringe of the jungle.

"Lousy traitor," Cable said, raising his rifle.

Sorensen slapped the muzzle of the rifle aside. "Don't do it."

"But he's helping that bug!"

"He can't help it," Sorensen said. "And he's not armed. Leave him alone."

Eakins watched for a few moments, then melted back into the jungle.

The attack by the rats and crabs swept across half of the cleared space. Then, as they came closer, the men were able to pick their targets with more accuracy. Nothing was able to get closer than twenty yards. And when Recetich shot down the bird of paradise, the attack began to falter.

"You know," Drake said, "I think we're going to be all right."

"Could be," said Sorensen. "I don't understand what the Quedak is trying to accomplish. He knows we can't be taken like this. I should think—"

"Hey!" one of the men called out. "Our boat!"

They turned and saw why the Quedak had ordered the attack. While it had occupied their attention, Drake's dog had swum out to the ketch and gnawed through the anchor line. Unattended, the ketch was drifting before the wind, moving toward the reef. They saw it bump gently, then harder. In a moment it was heeled hard over, stuck in the coral.

There was a burst of static from the walkie-talkie. Sorensen held it up and heard the Quedak say, "The ketch isn't seriously damaged. It's simply immobilized."

"The hell you say," Drake growled. "For all you know, it's got a whole punched right through it. How do you plan on getting off the island, Quedak? Or are you just going to stay here?"

"I will leave at the proper time," the Quedak said. "I want to make sure that we all leave together."

V

The wind died. Huge gray thunderheads piled up in the sky to the southeast, their tops lost in the upper atmosphere, their black anvil bottoms pressing the hot still air upon the island. The sun had lost its fiery glare. Cherry-red, it slid listlessly toward the flat sea.

High overhead, a single bird of paradise circled, just out of rifle range. It had gone up ten minutes after Recetich had shot the first one down.

Monty Byrnes stood on the edge of the cleared area, his rifle ready. He had drawn the first guard shift. The rest of the men were eating a hasty dinner inside the copra shed. Sorensen and Drake were outside, looking over the situation.

Drake said, "By nightfall we'll have to pull everybody back into the shed. Can't take a chance on being exposed to the Quedak in the dark."

Sorensen nodded. He seemed to have aged ten years in a day's time.

"In the morning," Drake said, "we'll be able to work something out. We'll . . . What's wrong, Bill?"

"Do you really think we have a chance?" Sorensen asked.

"Sure we do. We've got a damned good chance."

"Be realistic," Sorensen said. "The longer this goes on, the more animals the Quedak can throw against us. What can we do about it?"

"Hunt him out and kill him."

"The damned thing is about the size of your thumb," Sorensen said irritably. "How can we hunt him?"

"We'll figure out something," Drake said. He was beginning to get worried about Sorensen. The morale among the men was low enough without Sorensen pushing it down further.

"I wish someone would shoot that damned bird," Sorensen said, glancing overhead.

About every fifteen minutes, the bird of paradise came darting down for a closer look at the camp. Then, before the guard had a chance to fire, he swept back up to a safe altitude.

"It's getting on my nerves, too," Drake said. "Maybe that's what it's supposed to do. One of these times we'll—"

He stopped abruptly. From the copra shed he could hear the loud hum of a radio. And he heard Al Cable saying, "Hello, hello, this is Vuanu calling. We need help."

Drake and Sorensen went into the shed. Cable was sitting in front of the transmitter, saying into the microphone, "Emergency, emergency, Vuanu calling, we need—"

"What in hell do you think you're doing?" Drake snapped.

Cable turned and looked at him, his pudgy pink body

streaked with sweat. "I'm radioing for help, that's what I'm doing. I think I've picked up somebody. But they haven't answered me yet."

He readjusted the tuning. Over the receiver, they could hear a bored British voice saying, "Pawn to queen four, eh? Why don't you ever try a different opening?"

There was a sharp burst of static. "Just move," a deep bass voice answered. "Just shut up and move."

"Sure," said the British voice. "Knight to king bishop three."

Drake recognized the voices. They were ham radio operators. One of them owned a plantation on Bougainville; the other was a shopkeeper in Rabaul. They came on the air for an hour of chess and argument every evening.

Cable tapped the microphone impatiently. "Hello," he said, "this is Vuanu calling, emergency call—"

Drake walked over and took the microphone out of Cable's hand. He put it down carefully.

"We can't call for help," he said.

"What are you talking about?" Cable cried. "We have to!"

Drake felt very tired. "Look, if we send out a distress call, somebody's going to come sailing right in—but they won't be prepared for this kind of trouble. The Quedak will take them over and then use them against us."

"We can explain what the trouble is," Cable said.

"*Explain?* Explain *what?* That a bug is taking over the island? They'd think we were crazy with fever. They'd send in a doctor on the inter-island schooner."

"Dan's right," Sorensen said. "Nobody would believe this without seeing it for himself."

"And by then," Drake said, "it'd be too late. Eakins figured it out before the Quedak got him. That's why he told us not to send any messages."

Cable looked dubious. "But why did he want us to take the transmitter?"

"So that *he* couldn't send any messages after the bug got him," Drake said. "The more people trampling around, the easier it would be for the Quedak. If he had possession of the transmitter, he'd be calling for help right now."

"Yeah, I suppose so," Cable said unhappily. "But, damn it, we can't handle this *alone*."

"We have to. If the Quedak ever gets us and then gets off the island, that's it for Earth. Period. There won't be any big war, no hydrogen bombs or fallout, no heroic little resistance groups. Everybody will become part of the Quedak Co-operation."

"We ought to get help somehow," Cable said stubbornly. "We're alone, isolated. Suppose we ask for a ship to stand offshore—"

"It won't work," Drake said. "Besides, we couldn't ask for help even if we wanted to."

"Why not?"

"Because the transmitter's not working," Drake said. "You've been talking into a dead mike."

"It's receiving OK," Cable said.

Drake checked to see if all the switches were on. "Nothing wrong with the receiver. But we must have joggled something taking the transmitter out of the ship. It isn't working."

Cable tapped the dead microphone several times, then put it down. They stood around the receiver, listening to the chess game between the man in Rabaul and the man in Bougainville.

"Pawn to queen bishop four."

"Pawn to king three."

"Knight to queen bishop three."

There was a sudden staccato burst of static. It faded, then came again in three distinct bursts.

"What do you suppose that is?" Sorensen asked.

Drake shrugged his shoulders. "Could be anything. Storm's shaping up and—"

He stopped. He had been standing beside the door of the shed. As the static crackled, he saw the bird of paradise dive for a closer look. The static stopped when the bird returned to its slow-circling higher altitude.

"That's strange," Drake said. "Did you see that, Bill? The bird came down and the static went on at the same time."

"I saw it," Sorensen said. "Think it means anything?"

"I don't know. Let's see." Drake took out his field glasses. He turned up the volume of the receiver and stepped outside where he could observe the jungle. He waited, hearing the sounds of the chess game three or four hundred miles away.

"Come on now, move."

"Give me a minute."

"A minute? Listen, I can't stand in front of this bleeding set all night. Make your—"

Static crackled sharply. Drake saw four wild pigs come trotting out of the jungle, moving slowly, like a reconnaissance squad probing for weak spots in an enemy position. They stopped; the static stopped. Byrnes, standing guard with his rifle, took a snap shot at them. The pigs turned, and static crackled as they moved back into the jungle. There was more static as the bird of paradise swept down for a look, then climbed out of range. After that, the static stopped.

Drake put down his binoculars and went back inside the shed. "That must be it," he said. "The static is related to the Quedak. I think it comes when he's operating the animals."

"You mean he has some sort of radio control over them?" Sorensen asked.

"Seems like it," Drake said. "Either radio control or something propagated along a radio wave-length."

"If that's the case," Sorenson said, "he's like a little radio station, isn't he?"

"Sure he is. So what?"

"Then we should be able to locate him on a radio direction finder," Sorensen said.

Drake nodded emphatically. He snapped off the receiver, went to a corner of the shed and took out one of their portable direction finders. He set it to the frequency at which Cable had picked up the Rabaul-Bougainville broadcast. Then he turned it on and walked to the door.

The men watched while Drake rotated the loop antenna. He located the maximum signal, then turned the loop slowly, read the bearing and converted it to a compass course. Then he sat down with a small-scale chart of the Southwest Pacific.

"Well," Sorensen asked, "is it the Quedak?"

"It's got to be," said Drake. "I located a good null almost due south. That's straight ahead in the jungle."

"You're sure it isn't a reciprocal bearing?"

"I checked that out."

"Is there any chance the signal comes from some other station?"

"Nope. Due south, the next station is Sydney, and that's seventeen hundred miles away. Much too far for this RDF. It's the Quedak, all right."

"So we have a way of locating him," Sorensen said. "Two men with direction finders can go into the jungle—"

"—and get themselves killed," Drake said. "We can positon the Quedak with RDFs, but his animals can locate us a lot faster. We wouldn't have a chance in the jungle."

Sorensen looked crestfallen. "Then we're no better off than before."

"We're a lot better off," Drake said. "We have a chance now."

"What makes you think so?"

"He controls the animals by radio," Drake said. "We know the frequency he operates on. We can broadcast on the same frequency. We can jam his signal."

"Are you sure about that?"

"Am I *sure*? Of course not. But I do know that two stations in the same area can't broadcast over the same frequency. If we tuned in to the frequency the Quedak uses, made enough noise to override his signal—"

"I see," Sorensen said. "Maybe it would work! If we could interfere with his signal, he wouldn't be able to control the animals. And then we could hunt him down with the RDFs."

"That's the idea," Drake said. "It has only one small flaw —our transmitter isn't working. With no transmitter, we can't do any broadcasting. No broadcasting, no jamming."

"Can you fix it?" Sorensen asked.

"I'll try," Drake said. "But we'd better not hope for too much. Eakins was the radio man on this expedition."

"We've got all the spare parts," Sorensen said. "Tubes, manual, everything."

"I know. Give me enough time and I'll figure out what's wrong. The question is, how much time is the Quedak going to give us?"

The bright copper disk of the sun was half submerged in the sea. Sunset colors touched the massing thunderheads and faded into the brief tropical twilight. The men began to barricade the copra shed for the night.

VI

Drake removed the back from the transmitter and scowled at the compact mass of tubes and wiring. Those metal box-like things were probably condensers, and the waxy cylindrical gadgets might or might not be resistors. It all looked hopelessly complicated, ridiculously dense and delicate. Where should he begin?

He turned on the set and waited a few minutes. All the tubes appeared to go on, some dim, some bright. He couldn't detect any loose wires. The mike was still dead.

So much for visual inspection. Next question: was the set getting enough juice?

He turned it off and checked the battery cells with a voltmeter. The batteries were up to charge. He removed the leads, scraped them and put them back on, making sure they fit snugly. He checked all connections, murmured a propitiatory prayer, and turned the set on.

It still didn't work.

Cursing, he turned it off again. He decided to replace all the tubes, starting with the dim ones. If that didn't work, he could try replacing condensers and resistors. If that didn't work, he could always shoot himself. With this cheerful thought, he opened the parts kit and went to work.

The men were all inside the copra shed, finishing the job of barricading it for the night. The door was wedged shut and locked. The two windows had to be kept open for ventilation; otherwise everyone would suffocate in the heat. But a double layer of heavy mosquito netting was nailed over each window, and a guard was posted beside it.

Nothing could get through the flat galvanized-iron roof. The floor was of pounded earth, a possible danger point. All they could do was keep watch over it.

The treasure-hunters settled down for a long night. Drake, with a handkerchief tied around his forehead to keep the perspiration out of his eyes, continued working on the transmitter.

An hour later, there was a buzz on the walkie-talkie. Sorensen picked it up and said, "What do you want?"

"I want you to end this senseless resistance," said the Quedak, speaking with Eakins' voice. "You've had enough time to think over the situation. I want you to join me. Surely you can see there's no other way."

"We don't want to join you," Sorensen said.

"You must," the Quedak told him.

"Are you going to make us?"

"That poses problems," the Quedak said. "My animal parts are not suitable for coercion. Eakins is an excellent mechanism, but there is only one of him. And I must not expose myself to unnecessary danger. By doing so I would endanger the Quedak Mission."

"So it's a stalemate," Sorensen said.

"No. I am faced with difficulty only in taking you over. There is no problem in killing you."

The men shifted uneasily. Drake, working on the transmitter, didn't look up.

"I would rather *not* kill you," the Quedak said. "But the Quedak Mission is of primary importance. It would be endangered if you didn't join. It would be seriously compromised if you left the island. So you must either join or be killed."

"That's not the way I see it," Sorensen said. "If you killed us—assuming that you can—you'd never get off this island. Eakins can't handle that ketch."

"There would be no need to leave in the ketch," the Quedak said. "In six months, the inter-island schooner will return. Eakins and I will leave then. The rest of you will have died."

"You're bluffing," Sorensen said. "What makes you think you could kill us? You didn't do so well today." He caught Drake's attention and gestured at the radio. Drake shrugged his shoulders and went back to work.

"I wasn't trying," the Quedak said. "The time for that was at night. *This* night, before you have a chance to work out a better system of defense. You must join me tonight or I will kill one of you."

"One of us?"

"Yes. One man an hour. In that way, perhaps the survivors will change their minds about joining. But if they don't, all of you will be dead by morning."

Drake leaned over and whispered to Sorensen, "Stall him. Give me another ten minutes. I think I've found the trouble."

Sorensen said into the walkie-talkie, "We'd like to know a little more about the Quedak Cooperation."

"You can find out best by joining."

"We'd rather have a little more information on it first."

"It is an indescribable state," the Quedak said in an urgent, earnest, eager voice. "Can you imagine yourself as *yourself* and yet experiencing an entirely new series of sensory networks? You would, for example, experience the world through the perceptors of a dog as he goes through the forest following an odor which to him—and to you—is as clear and vivid as a painted line. A hermit crab senses things differently. From him you experience the slow interaction of life at the margin of sea and land. His time-sense is very slow, unlike that of a bird of paradise, whose viewpoint is spatial, rapid, cursory. And there are many others, above and below the earth and water, who furnish their own specialized viewpoints of reality. Their outlooks, I have found, are not essentially different from those of the animals that once inhabited Mars."

"What happened on Mars?" Sorensen asked.

"All life died," the Quedak mourned. "All except the Quedak. It happened a long time ago. For centuries there was peace and prosperity on the planet. Everything and everyone was part of the Quedak Cooperation. But the dominant race was basically weak. Their breeding rate went down; catastrophes happened. And finally there was no more life except the Quedak."

"Sounds great," Sorensen said ironically.

"It was the fault of the race," the Quedak protested. "With sturdier stock—such as you have on this planet—the will to live will remain intact. The peace and prosperity will continue indefinitely."

"I don't believe it. What happened on Mars will happen again on Earth if you take over. After a while, slaves just don't care very strongly about living."

"You wouldn't be slaves. You would be functional parts of the Quedak Cooperation."

"Which would be run by you," Sorensen said. "Any way you slice it, it's the same old pie."

"You don't know what you're talking about," the Quedak said. "We have talked long enough. I am prepared to kill one man in the next five minutes. Are you or are you not going to join me?" Sorensen looked at Drake. Drake turned on the transmitter.

Gusts of rain splattered on the roof while the transmitter warmed up. Drake lifted the microphone and tapped it, and was able to hear the sound in the speaker.

"It's working," he said.

At that moment something flew against the netting-covered window. The netting sagged; a fruit bat was entangled in it, glaring at them with tiny red-rimmed eyes.

"Get some boards over that window!" Sorensen shouted.

As he spoke, a second bat hurtled into the netting, broke through it and tumbled to the floor. The men clubbed it to death, but four more bats flew in through the open window. Drake flailed at them, but he couldn't drive them away from the transmitter. They were diving at his eyes, and he was forced back. A wild blow caught one bat and knocked it to the floor with a broken wing. Then the others had reached the transmitter.

They pushed it off the table. Drake tried to catch the set, and failed. He heard the glass tubes shattering, but by then he was busy protecting his eyes.

In a few minutes they had killed two more bats, and the others had fled out the window. The men nailed boards over both windows, and Drake bent to examine the transmitter.

"Any chance of fixing it?" Sorensen asked.

"Not a hope," Drake said. "They ripped out the wiring while they were at it."

"What do we do now?"

"I don't know."

Then the Quedak spoke to them over the walkie-talkie. "I must have your answer right now."

Nobody said a word.

"In that case," the Quedak said, "I'm deeply sorry that one of you must die now."

VII

Rain pelted the iron roof and the gusts of wind increased in intensity. There were rumbles of distant thunder. But within the copra shed, the air was hot and still. The gasoline lantern hanging from the center beam threw a harsh yellow light that illuminated the center of the room but left the corners in deep shadow. The treasure-hunters had moved away from the walls. They were all in the center of the room facing outward, and they made Drake think of a herd of buffalo drawn up against a wolf they could smell but could not see.

Cable said, "Listen, maybe we should try this Quedak Cooperation. Maybe it isn't so bad as—"

"Shut up," Drake said.

"Be reasonable," Cable argued. "It's better than dying, isn't it?"

"No one's dying yet," Drake said. "Just shut up and keep your eyes open."

"I think I'm going to be sick," Cable said. "Dan, let me out."

"Be sick where you are," Drake said. "Just keep your eyes open."

"You can't give me orders," Cable said. He started toward the door. Then he jumped back.

A yellowish scorpion had crept under the inch of clearance between the door and the floor. Recetich stamped on it, smashing it to pulp under his heavy boots. Then he whirled, swinging at three hornets which had come at him through the boarded windows.

"Forget the hornets!" Drake shouted. "Keep watching the ground!"

There was movement on the floor. Several hairy spiders crawled out of the shadows. Drake and Recetich beat at them with rifle butts. Byrnes saw something crawling under the door. It looked like some kind of huge flat centipede. He stamped at it, missed, and the centipede was on his boot, past it, on the flesh of his leg. He screamed; it felt like a ribbon of molten metal. He was able to smash it flat before he passed out.

Drake checked the wound and decided it was not fatal. He stamped on another spider, then felt Sorensen's hand clutching his shoulder. He looked toward the corner Sorensen was pointing at.

Sliding toward them were two large, dark-coated snakes. Drake recognized them as black adders. These normally shy creatures were coming forward like tigers.

The men panicked, trying to get away from the snakes. Drake pulled out his revolver and dropped to one knee, ignoring the hornets that buzzed around him, trying to draw a bead on the slender serpentine targets in the swaying yellow light.

Thunder roared directly overhead. A long flash of lightning suddenly flooded the room, spoiling his aim. Drake fired and missed, and waited for the snakes to strike.

They didn't strike. They were moving away from him, retreating to the rat hole from which they had emerged. One of the adders slid quickly through. The other began to follow, then stopped, half in the hole.

Sorensen took careful aim with a rifle. Drake pushed the muzzle aside. "Wait just a moment."

The adder hesitated. It came out of the hole and began to move toward them again . . .

And there was another crash of thunder and a vivid splash of lightning. The snake turned away and squirmed through the hole.

"What's going on?" Sorensen asked. "Is the thunder frightening them?"

"No, it's the lightning!" Drake said. "That's why the Quedak was in such a rush. He saw that a storm was coming, and he hadn't consolidated his position yet."

"What are you talking about?"

"The lightning," Drake said. "The electrical storm! It's jamming that radio control of his! And when he's jammed, the beasts revert to normal behavior. It takes him time to re-establish control."

"The storm won't last forever," Cable said.

"But maybe it'll last long enough," Drake said. He picked up the direction finders and handed one to Sorensen. "Come on, Bill. We'll hunt out that bug right now."

"Hey," Recetich said, "isn't there something I can do?"

"You can start swimming if we don't come back in an hour," Drake said.

In slanting lines the rain drove down, pushed by the wild southwest wind. Thunder rolled continually and each flash of lightning seemed aimed at them. Drake and Sorensen reached the edge of the jungle and stopped.

"We'll separate here," Drake said. "Gives us a better chance of converging on him."

"Right," Sorensen said. "Take care of yourself, Dan."

Sorensen plunged into the jungle. Drake trotted fifty yards down the fringe and then entered the bush.

He pushed forward, the revolver in his belt, the radio direction finder in one hand, a flashlight in the other. The jungle seemed to be animated by a vicious life of its own, almost as if the Quedak controlled it. Vines curled cunningly around his ankles and the bushes reached out thorny hands toward him. Every branch took a special delight in slapping his face.

Each time the lightning flashed, Drake's direction finder tried to home on it. He was having a difficult time staying on course. But, he reminded himself, the Quedak was undoubtedly having an even more difficult time. Between flashes, he was able to set a course. The further he penetrated into the jungle, the stronger the signal became.

After a while he noticed that the flashes of lightning were spaced more widely apart. The storm was moving on toward the north, leaving the island behind. How much longer would he have the protection of the lightning? Another ten or fifteen minutes?

He heard something whimper. He swung his flashlight around and saw his dog, Oro, coming toward him.

His dog—or the Quedak's dog?

"Hey there, boy," Drake said. He wondered if he should

drop the direction finder and get the revolver out of his belt. He wondered if the revolver would still work after such a thorough soaking.

Oro came up and licked his hand. He was Drake's dog, at least for the duration of the storm.

They moved on together, and the thunder rumbled distantly in the north. The signal on his RDF was very strong now. Somewhere around here . . .

He saw light from another flashlight. Sorensen, badly out of breath, had joined him. The jungle had ripped and clawed at him, but he still had his rifle, flashlight and direction finder.

Oro was scratching furiously at a bush. There was a long flash of lightning, and in it they saw the Quedak.

Drake realized, in those final moments, that the rain had stopped. The lightning had stopped, too. He dropped the direction finder. With the flashlight in one hand and his revolver in the other, he tried to take aim at the Quedak, who was moving, who had jumped—

To Sorensen's neck, just above the right collarbone.

Sorensen raised his hands, then lowered them again. He turned toward Drake, raising his rifle. His face was perfectly calm. He looked as though his only purpose in life was to kill Drake.

Drake fired from less than two feet away. Sorensen spun with the impact, dropped his rifle and fell.

Drake bent over him, his revolver ready. He saw that he had fired accurately. The bullet had gone in just above the right collarbone. It was a bad wound. But it had been much worse for the Quedak, who had been in the direct path of the bullet. All that was left of the Quedak was a splatter of black across Sorensen's chest.

Drake applied hasty first aid and hoisted Sorensen to his shoulders. He wondered what he would have done if the Quedak had been standing above Sorensen's heart, or on his throat, or on his head.

He decided it was better not to think about that.

He started back to camp, with his dog trotting along beside him.

POTENTIAL

HE returned to conscious-
ness slowly, aware of aches and bruises, and an agonizing
knot in his stomach. Experimentally, he stretched his legs.

They didn't touch anything, and he realized that his body
was unsupported. He was dead, he thought. Floating free
in space—

Floating? He opened his eyes. Yes, he was floating. Above
him was a ceiling—or was it a floor? He resisted a strong
urge to scream; blinked, and his surroundings swam into
focus.

He realized that he was in a spaceship. The cabin was a
shambles. Boxes and equipment drifted around him, evidently
ripped loose from their moorings by some sudden strain.
Burnt-out wires ran across the floor. A row of lockers along
one wall had been fused into slag.

He stared, but no recognition came. As far as he knew, he
was seeing this for the first time. He raised a hand and pushed
against the ceiling, drifted down, pushed again, and managed
to grasp a wall rail. Holding this tightly, he tried to think.

"There is a logical explanation for all this," he said aloud,
just to hear his own voice. "All I have to do is remember."
Remember—

What was his name?

He didn't know.

"Hello!" he shouted. "Is there anyone here?" His words
echoed between the ship's narrow walls. There was no
answer.

He propelled himself across the cabin, ducking to miss the

floating boxes. In half an hour he knew he was the only person aboard the ship.

He pushed himself back to the front of the ship. There was a padded chair there, with a long panel in front of it. He strapped himself into the chair and studied the panel.

It consisted of two blank screens, one much larger than the other. Under the large screen were two buttons, marked *vision-front,* and *vision-back.* A dial beneath the buttons was calibrated for focus. The small screen was unmarked.

Not finding any other controls, he pushed the *vision-front* button. The screen cleared, showing black space with the brilliant points of the stars before him. He stared at it for a long time, open-mouthed, then turned away.

The first thing to do, he told himself, was to assemble all the knowledge at his disposal and see what he could deduce from it.

"I am a man," he said. "I am in a spaceship, in space. I know what stars are, and what planets are. Let me see—" He had a rudimentary knowledge of astronomy, less of physics and chemistry. He remembered some English literature, although he couldn't think of any writers except Traudzel, a popular novelist. He remembered the authors of several history books, but couldn't place their contents.

He knew the name for what he had: amnesia.

Suddenly, he had a great desire to see himself, to look at his own face. Surely, recognition and memory would follow. He shoved himself across the room again, and started searching for a mirror.

There were lockers built into the walls, and he opened them hastily, spilling the contents into the weightless air. In the third locker he found a shaving kit and a small steel mirror. He studied the reflection anxiously.

A long irregular face, drained of color. Dark stubble growing on the chin. Bloodless lips.

The face of a stranger.

He fought down fresh panic and searched the cabin, looking for some clue to his identity. Quickly he pawed through the floating boxes, shoving them aside when they proved to contain nothing but food or water. He looked on.

Floating in one corner of the cabin was a sheet of scorched paper. He seized it.

"Dear Ran," it began. "The biochem boys have been

doing some hurry-hurry last-minute checking on the pento. Seems there's a strong chance it might induce amnesia. Something about the strength of the drug, plus the near-traumatic experience you're undergoing, whether you're aware of it or not. *Now* they tell us! Anyhow, I'm dashing off this note at zero minus fourteen minutes, just as a refresher for you in case they're right.

"First, don't look for any controls. Everything's automatic, or it should be if this pile of cardboard and glue holds together. (Don't blame the technicians; they had practically no time to get it finished and away before flash moment).

"Your course is set for automatic planetary selection, so just sit tight. I don't suppose you could forget Marselli's theorem, but in case you have, don't worry about landing among some eighteen-headed intelligent centipedes. You'll reach humanoid life because it *has* to be humanoid life.

"You may be a bit battered after blastoff, but the pento will pull you through. If the cabin is messy, it's because we just didn't have time to check everything for stress-strain tolerances.

"Now for the mission. Go at once to Projector One in Locker Fifteen. The projector is set for self-destruction after one viewing, so make sure you understand it. The mission is of ultimate importance, Doc, and every man and woman on Earth is with you. Don't let us down."

Someone named Fred Anderson had signed it.

Ran—automatically using the name given in the letter— started looking for Locker Fifteen. He found at once where it had been. Lockers Eleven through Twenty-five were fused and melted. Their contents were destroyed.

That was that. Only the scorched paper linked him now with his past, his friends, all Earth. Even though his memory was gone, it was a relief to know that the amnesia had an explanation.

But what did it mean? Why had they thrown the ship together in such a rush? Why had they placed him in it— alone—and sent him out? And this all-important mission— if it was so vital, why hadn't they safeguarded it better?

The note raised more questions than it answered. Frowning, Ran pushed himself back to the panel. He looked out the screen again, at the spectacle of the stars, trying to reason it out.

Perhaps there was a disease. He was the only person not

infected. They had built the ship and shot him out to space.
The mission? To contact another planet, find an antidote,
and bring it back—

Ridiculous.

He looked over the panel again, and pushed the button
for *vision-rear*.

And almost fainted.

A glaring, blinding light filled the entire screen, scorching
his eyes. Hastily he cut down the field of focus, until he was
able to make out what it was.

A nova. And the letter had mentioned the flash-moment.

Ran knew that Sol was the nova. And that Earth was
consumed.

There was no clock on the ship, so Dr. Ran had no idea
how long he had been traveling. For a long time he just
drifted around dazed, coming back to the screen constantly.

The nova dwindled as the ship speeded on.

Ran ate and slept. He wandered around the ship, examining, searching. The floating boxes were in the way, so he
started to pull them down and secure them.

Days might have passed, or weeks.

After a while, Ran started to put the facts he knew into a
coherent structure. There were gaps and questions in it,
probably untruths as well, but it was a beginning.

He had been chosen to go in the spaceship. Not as a pilot,
since the ship was automatic, but for some other reason. The
letter had called him "Doc". It might have something to do
with his being a doctor.

Doctor of what? He didn't know.

The makers of the ship had known Sol was going nova.
They couldn't, evidently, rescue any sizable portion of
Earth's population. Instead, they had sacrificed themselves
and everyone else to make sure of rescuing him.

Why him?

He was expected to do a job of the greatest importance.
So important that everyone had been subordinated to it.
So important that the destruction of Earth itself seemed
secondary, as long as the mission was accomplished.

What could that mission be?

Dr. Ran couldn't conceive of anything so important. But
he had no other theory that came even close to fitting the
facts as he knew them.

He tried to attack the problem from another viewpoint.

What would he do, he asked himself, if he knew that Sol was going nova in a short time, and he could rescue only a limited number of people with a certainty of success?

He would have sent out couples, at least one couple, in an attempt to perpetuate human stock.

But evidently the leaders of Earth hadn't seen it that way.

After a time, the small screen flashed into life. It read: *Planet. Contact 100 hours.*

He sat in front of the panel and watched. After a long time the digits changed. *Contact 99 hours.*

He had plenty of time. He ate, and went back to work getting the ship into what order he could.

While he was storing boxes in the remaining lockers, he found a carefully packaged and fastened machine. He recognized it as a projector at once. On its side was engraved a large "2".

A spare, he thought, his heart pounding violently. Why hadn't he thought of that? He looked into the viewer and pushed the button.

The film took over an hour. It started with a poetic survey of Earth; flashes of her cities, fields, forests, rivers, oceans. Her people, her animals, all in brief vignettes. There was no sound track.

The camera moved to an observatory, explaining its purpose visually. It showed the discovery of the Sun's instability, the faces of the astrophysicists who discovered it.

Then the race against time began, and the rapid growth of the ship. He saw himself, running up to it, grinning at the camera, shaking someone's hand, and disappearing inside. The film stopped there. They must have stored the camera, given him the injection, and sent him off.

Another reel started.

"Hello, Ran," a voice said. The picture showed a large, calm man in a business suit. He looked directly at Ran out of the screen.

"I couldn't resist this opportunity to speak to you again, Dr. Ellis. You're deep in space now, and you've undoubtedly seen the nova that has consumed Earth. You're lonely, I dare say.

"Don't be, Ran. As representative of Earth's peoples, I'm taking this final chance to wish you luck in your great mission. I don't have to tell you that we're all with you. Don't feel alone."

"You have, of course, seen the film in Projector One, and have a thorough understanding of your mission. This portion of film—with my face and voice on it—will be automatically destroyed, in the same way. Naturally, we can't let extraterrestrials in on our little secret yet.

"They'll find out soon enough. You can feel free to explain anything on the remainder of this film to them. It should win you plenty of sympathy. Make no reference, of course, to the great discovery or the techniques that stemmed from it. If they want the faster-than-light drive, tell them the truth—that you don't know how it's propagated, since it was developed only a year or so before Sol went nova. Tell them that any tampering with the ship will cause the engines to dissolve.

"Good luck, doctor. And good hunting." The face faded and the machine hummed louder, destroying the last reel.

He put the projector carefully back in its case, tied it into the locker, and went back to the control panel.

The screen read: *Contact 97 hours.*

He sat down and tried to place the new facts into his structure. As background, he remembered vaguely the great, peaceful civilization of Earth. They had been almost ready to go for the stars when the Sun's instability was found. The faster-than-light drive had been developed too late.

Against that background he had been selected to man the escape ship. Only him, for some unfathomable reason. The job given him was thought more important, evidently, than any attempts at race-survival.

He was to make contact with intelligent life, and tell them about Earth. But he was to withhold any mention of the greatest discovery and its resulting techniques.

Whatever they were.

And then he was to perform his mission—

He felt as though he could burst. He couldn't remember. *Why* hadn't the fools engraved his instructions on bronze? *What could it be?*

The screen read, *Contact 96 hours.*

Dr. Ran Ellis strapped himself into the pilot chair and cried from sheer frustration.

The great ship looked, probed and reported. The small screen flashed into life. *Atmosphere-chlorine. Life-nonexistent.* The data was fed to the ship's selectors. Circuits closed, other circuits opened. A new course was set up, and the ship speeded on.

Dr. Ellis ate and slept and thought.

Another planet was reported, examined and rejected.

Dr. Ellis continued thinking, and made one unimportant discovery.

He had a photographic memory. He discovered this by thinking back over the film. He could remember every detail of the hour-long spectacle, every face, every movement.

He tested himself as the ship went on, and found that the ability was a constant. It worried him for a while, until he realized that it was probably a factor in his selection. A photographic memory would be quite an asset in learning a new language.

Quite an irony, he thought. Perfect retention—but no memory.

A third planet was rejected.

Ellis outlined the possibilities he could think of, in an effort to discover the nature of his mission.

To erect a shrine to Earth? Possibly. But why the urgency, then, the stressed importance?

Perhaps he was sent out as a teacher. Earth's last gesture, to instruct some inhabitated planet in the ways of peace and cooperation.

Why send a doctor on a job like that? Besides, it was illogical. People learn over millennia, not in a few years. And it just didn't fit the *mood* of the two messages. Both the man in the film and the note-writer had seemed practical men. It was impossible to think of either of them as altruists.

A fourth planet came into range, was checked and left behind.

And what, he wondered, was the "great discovery"? If not the faster-than-light drive, what could it be? More than likely a philosophical discovery. The way man could live in peace, or something like that.

Then why wasn't he supposed to mention it?

A screen flashed, showing the oxygen content of the fifth planet. Ellis ignored it, then looked up as generators deep in the body of the ship hummed into life.

Prepare for landing, the screen told him.

His heart leaped convulsively, and Ellis had a momentary difficulty breathing.

This was it. A terror filled him as gravitation tugged at

the ship. He fought it, but the terror increased. He screamed and tore at his straps as the ship started to go perceptibly *down*.

On the big screen was the blue and green of an oxygen planet.

Then Ellis remembered something. "The emergence from deep space into a planetary system is analogous to the emergent birth-trauma." A common reaction, he told himself, but an easily controllable one for a psychiatrist—

A psychiatrist!

Dr. Randolph Ellis, psychiatrist. He knew what kind of doctor he was. He searched his mind for more information, fruitlessly. That was as far as it went.

Why had Earth sent a psychiatrist into space?

He blacked out as the ship screamed into the atmosphere.

Ellis recovered almost at once as the ship landed itself. Unstrapping, he switched on the vision-ports. There were vehicles coming toward the ship, filled with people.

Human-appearing people.

He had to make a decision now, one that would affect the rest of his time on this planet. What was he going to do? What would his course of action be?

Ellis thought for a moment, then decided he would have to play by ear. He would extemporize. No communication would be possible until he had learned the language. After that, he would say that he was sent from Earth to . . . to—

What?

He would decide when the time came. Glancing at the screens, he saw that the atmosphere was breathable.

The side of the ship swung open, and Ellis walked out.

He had landed on a subcontinent called Kreld, and the inhabitants were Kreldans. Politically, the planet had reached the world-government stage, but so recently that the inhabitants still were identified with the older political divisions.

With his photographic memory Ellis found no difficulty learning the Kreldan language, once a common basis had been established for key words. The people, of the common root Man, seemed no more foreign than some members of his own race. Ellis knew that this eventuality had been predicted. The ship would have rejected any other. The more he thought of it, the more he was certain that the mission depended on this similarity.

Ellis learned and observed, and thought. He was due, as soon as he had mastered the tongue sufficiently, to meet the ruling council. This was a meeting he dreaded, and put off as long as he could.

Nevertheless, the time came.

He was ushered through the halls of the Council Building, to the door of the Main Council Room. He walked in with the projector under his arm.

"You are most welcome, sir," the leader of the council said. Ellis returned the salutation and presented his films. There was no discussion until everyone had seen them.

"Then you are the last representative of your race?" the council leader asked. Ellis nodded, looking at the kindly, seamed old face.

"Why did your people send only you?" another council member asked. "Why weren't a man and woman sent?" The same question, Ellis thought, that I've been asking myself.

"It would be impossible," he told them, "for me to explain the psychology of my race in a few words. Our decision was contained in our very sense of being." A meaningless lie, he thought to himself. But what else could he say?

"You will have to explain the psychology of your race sometime," the man said.

Ellis nodded, looking over the faces of the council. He was able to estimate the effect of the beautifully prepared film on them; they were going to be pleasant to this last representative of a great race.

"We are very interested in your faster-than-light drive," another council member said. "Could you help us attain that?"

"I'm afraid not," Ellis said. From what he had learned, he knew that their technology was pre-atomic, several centuries behind Earth's.

"I am not a scientist. I have no knowledge of the drive. It was a late development."

"We could examine it ourselves," a man said.

"I don't think that would be wise," Ellis told him. "My people consider it inadvisable to give a planet technological products beyond their present level of attainment." So much for theory. "The engines will overload if tampered with."

"You say you are not a scientist," the old leader asked pleasantly, changing the subject. "If I may ask, what are you?"

"A psychiatrist," Ellis said.

They talked for hours. Ellis dodged and faked and invented, trying to fill in the gaps in his knowledge. The council wanted to know about all phases of life on Earth, all the details of technological and social advances. They wondered about Earth's method of pre-nova detection. And why had he decided to come here? And finally, in view of coming alone, was his race suicidally inclined?

"We will wish to ask you more in the future," the old council leader said, ending the session.

"I shall be happy to answer anything in my power," Ellis said.

"That doesn't seem to be much," a member said.

"Now Elgg—remember the shock this man has been through," the council leader said. "His entire race has been destroyed. I do not believe we are being hospitable." He turned to Ellis.

"Sir, you have helped us immeasurably as it is. For example, now that we know the possibility of controlled atomic power, we can direct research toward that goal. Of course, you will be reimbursed by the state. What would you like to do?"

Ellis hesitated, wondering what he should say.

"Would you like to head a museum project for Earth? A monument to your great people?"

Was that his mission, Ellis wondered? He shook his head.

"I am a doctor, sir. A psychiatrist. Perhaps I could help in that respect."

"But you don't know our people," the old leader said concernedly. "It would take you a lifetime to learn the nature of our tensions and problems. To learn them in sufficient intimacy to enable you to practice."

"True," Ellis said. "But our races *are* alike. Our civilizations have taken like courses. Since I represent a more advanced psychological tradition, my methods might be of help to your doctors—"

"Of course, Dr. Ellis. I must not make the mistake of underestimating a species that has crossed the stars." The old leader smiled ruefully. "I myself will introduce you to the head of one of our hospitals." The leader stood up.

"If you will come with me."

Ellis followed, with his heart pounding. His mission must have something to do with psychiatry. Why else send a psychiatrist?

But he still didn't know what he was supposed to do.

And, to make it worse, he could remember practically none of his psychiatric background.

"I think that takes care of all the testing apparatus," the doctor said, looking at Ellis from behind steel-rimmed glasses. He was young, moon-faced, and eager to learn from the older civilization of Earth.

"Can you suggest any improvements?" he asked.

"I'll have to look over the setup more closely," Ellis said, following the doctor down a long, pale-blue corridor. The testing apparatus had struck a complete blank.

"I don't have to tell you how eager I am for this opportunity," the doctor said. "I have no doubt that you Terrans were able to discover many of the secrets of the mind."

"Oh, yes," Ellis said.

"Down this way we have the wards," the doctor said. "Would you care to see them?"

"Fine." Ellis followed the doctor, biting his lip angrily. His memory was still gone. He had no more psychiatric knowledge than a poorly informed layman. Unless something happened soon, he would be forced to admit his amnesia.

"In this room," the doctor said, "we have several quiet cases." Ellis followed him in, and looked at the dull, lifeless faces of three patients.

"Catatonic," the doctor said, pointing to the first man. "I don't suppose you have a cure for that?" He smiled good-naturedly.

Ellis didn't answer. Another memory had popped into his mind. It was just a few lines of conversation.

"But is it ethical?" he had asked. In a room like this, on Earth.

"Of course," someone had answered. "We won't tamper with the normals. But the idiots, the criminally insane—the psychotics who could never use their minds anyhow—it isn't as though we were robbing them of anything. It's a mercy, really—"

Just that much. He didn't know to whom he had been talking. Another doctor, probably. They had been discussing some new method of dealing with defectives. A new cure? It seemed possible. A drastic one, from the content.

"Have you found a cure for it?" the moon-faced doctor asked again.

"Yes. Yes, we have," Ellis said, taking his nerve in both hands. The doctor stepped back and stared.

"But you couldn't! You can't repair a brain where there's organic damage—deterioration, or lack of development—" He checked himself.

"But listen to *me*, telling *you*. Go ahead, doctor."

Ellis looked at the man in the first bed. "Get me some assistants, doctor." The doctor hesitated, then hurried out of the room.

Ellis bent over the catatonic and looked at his face. He wasn't sure of what he was doing, but he reached out and touched the man's forehead with his finger.

Something in Ellis' mind clicked.

The catatonic collapsed.

Ellis waited, but nothing seemed to be happening. He walked over to the second patient and repeated the operation.

That one collapsed also, and the one after him.

The doctor came back, with two wide-eyed helpers. "What's happening here?" he asked. "What have you done?"

"I don't know if our methods will work on your people," Ellis bluffed. "Please leave me alone—completely alone for a little while. The concentration necessary—" He turned back to the patients.

The doctor started to say something, changed his mind and left quietly, taking the assistants with him.

Sweating, Ellis examined the pulse of the first man. It was still beating. He straightened and started to pace the room.

He had a power of some sort. He could knock a psychotic flat on his back. Fine. Nerves—connections. He wished he could remember how many nerve connections there were in the human brain. Some fantastic number; Ten to the twenty-fifth to the tenth? No, that didn't seem right. But a fantastic number.

What did it matter? It mattered, he was certain.

The first man groaned and sat up. Ellis walked over to him. The man felt his head, and groaned again.

His own personal shock-therapy, Ellis thought. Perhaps Earth had discovered the answer to insanity. As a last gift to the universe, they had sent him out, to heal—

"How do you feel?" he asked the patient.

"Not bad," the man answered—in English!

"What did you say?" Ellis gasped. He wondered if there had been a thought-transfer of some sort. Had he given the man his own grasp of English? Let's see, if you reshunted the load from the damaged nerves to unused ones—

"I feel fine, Doc. Good work. We weren't sure if that haywire and cardboard ship would hold together, but as I told you, it was the best we could do under the—"

"Who are you?"

The man climbed out of bed and looked around.

"Are the natives gone?"

"Yes."

"I'm Haines, Representative of Earth. What's the matter with you, Ellis?"

The other men were reviving now.

"And they—"

"Dr. Clitell."

"Fred Anderson."

The man who called himself Haines looked over his body carefully. "You might have found a better host for me, Ellis. For old time's sake. But no matter. What's the matter, man?"

Ellis explained about his amnesia.

"Didn't you get the note?"

Ellis told them everything.

"We'll get your memory back, don't worry," Haines said. "It feels good to have a body again. Hold it."

The door opened and the young doctor peered in. He saw the patients and let out a shout.

"You did it! You are able—"

"Please, doctor," Ellis snapped. "No sudden noises. I must ask not to be disturbed for at least another hour."

"Of course," the doctor said respectfully, withdrew his face and closed the door.

"How was it possible?" Ellis asked, looking at the three men. "I don't understand—"

"The great discovery," Haines said. "Surely you remember that? You worked on it. No? Explain, Anderson."

The third man walked over slowly. Ellis noticed that the vacuous faces were beginning to tighten already, shaped by the minds in back of them.

"Don't you remember, Ellis, the research on personality factors?"

Ellis shook his head.

"You were looking for the lowest common denominator of human-life-and-personality. The source, if you wish. The research actually started almost a hundred years ago, after Orgell found that personality was independent of body, although influenced and modified by it. Remember now?"

"No. Go on."

"To keep it simple, you—and about thirty others—found that the lowest indivisible unit of personality was an independent nonmaterial substance. You named it the M molecule. It is a complex mental pattern."

"Mental?"

"Nonmaterial, then," Anderson said. "It can be transferred from host to host."

"Sounds like possession," Ellis said.

Anderson, noticing a mirror in a corner of the room, walked over to examine his new face. He shuddered when he saw it, and wiped saliva from its lips.

"The old myths of spirit-possession aren't so far off," Dr. Clitell said. He was the only one wearing his body with any sort of ease. "Some people have always been able to separate their minds from their bodies. Astral projection, and that sort of thing. It wasn't until recently that the personality was localized and an invariant separation-resynthesis procedure adopted."

"Does that mean you're immortal?" Ellis asked.

"Oh, no!" Anderson said, walking over. He grimaced, trying to check his host's unconscious drool. "The personality has a definite life span. It's somewhat longer than the body's, of course, but still definitely within limits." He succeeded in stopping the flow. "However, it can be stored dormant almost indefinitely."

"And what better place," Haines put in, "for storing a nonmaterial molecule than your own mind? Your nerve connections have been harboring us all along, Ellis. There's plenty of room there. The number of connections in a human brain have been calculated at ten to the—"

"I remember that part," Ellis said. "I'm beginning to understand." He knew why he had been chosen. A psychiatrist would be needed for this job, to gain admittance to the hosts. He had been especially trained. Of course the Kreldans couldn't be told yet about the mission or the M molecule. They wouldn't take kindly to their people—even the defectives—being possessed by Earthmen.

"Look at this," Haines said. Fascinated, he was bending his fingers backwards. He had discovered that his host was double-jointed. The other two men were trying out their bodies in the manner of a man testing a horse. They flexed their arms, bunched their muscles, practiced walking.

"But," Ellis asked, "how will the race . . . I mean, how about women?"

"Get more hosts," Haines told him, still trying out his fingers. "Male and female. You're going to be the greatest doctor on this planet. Every defective will be brought to you for cure. Of course, we're all in on the secret. No one's going to spill before the right time." He paused and grinned. "Ellis —do you realize what this means? Earth isn't dead! She'll live again."

Ellis nodded. He was having difficulty identifying the large, bland Haines in the film with the shrill-voiced scarecrow in front of him. It would take time for all of them, he knew, and a good deal of readjustment.

"We'd better get to work," Anderson said. "After you have the defectives on this planet serviced, we'll refuel your ship and send you on."

"Where?" Ellis asked. "To another planet?"

"Of course. There are probably only a few million hosts on this one, since we're not touching normals."

"Only! But how many people have I stored?"

There was the sound of voices in the hall.

"You really are a case," Haines said, amused. "Back into bed, men—I think I hear that doctor. How many? The population of Earth was about four billion. You have all of them."

FOOL'S

MATE

THE players met, on the great, timeless board of space. The glittering dots that were the pieces swam in their separate patterns. In that configuration at the beginning, even before the first move was made, the outcome of the game was determined.

Both players saw, and knew which had won. But they played on.

Because the game had to be played out.

"Nielson!"

Lieutenant Nielson sat in front of his gunfire board with an idyllic smile on his face. He didn't look up.

"Nielson!"

The lieutenant was looking at his fingers now, with the stare of a puzzled child.

"Nielson! Snap out of it!" General Branch loomed sternly over him. "Do you hear me, lieutenant?"

Nielson shook his head dully. He started to look at his fingers again, then his gaze was caught by the glittering array of buttons on the gunfire panel.

"Pretty," he said.

General Branch stepped inside the cubicle, grabbed Nielson by the shoulders and shook him.

"Pretty things," Nielson said, gesturing at the panel. He smiled at Branch.

Margraves, second in command, stuck his head in the doorway. He still had sergeant's stripes on his sleeve, having been promoted to colonel only three days ago.

"Ed," he said, "the President's representative is here. Sneak visit."

"Wait a minute," Branch said, "I want to complete this inspection." He grinned sourly. It was one hell of an inspection when you went around finding how many sane men you had left.

"Do you hear me, lieutenant?"

"Ten thousand ships," Nielson said. "Ten thousand ships—all gone!"

"I'm sorry," Branch said. He leaned forward and slapped him smartly across the face.

Lieutenant Nielson started to cry.

"Hey, Ed—what about that representative?"

At close range, Colonel Margraves' breath was a solid essence of whisky, but Branch didn't reprimand him. If you had a good officer left you didn't reprimand him, no matter what he did. Also, Branch approved of whisky. It was a good release, under the circumstances. Probably better than his own, he thought, glancing at his scarred knuckles.

"I'll be right with you. Nielson, can you understand me?"

"Yes, sir," the lieutenant said in a shaky voice. "I'm all right now, sir."

"Good," Branch said. "Can you stay on duty?"

"For a while," Nielson said. "But, sir—I'm not well. I can feel it."

"I know," Branch said. "You deserve a rest. But you're the only gun officer I've got left on this side of the ship. The rest are in the wards."

"I'll try, sir," Nielson said, looking at the gunfire panel again. "But I hear voices sometimes. I can't promise anything, sir."

"Ed," Margraves began again, "that representative—"

"Coming. Good boy, Nielson." The lieutenant didn't look up as Branch and Margraves left.

"I escorted him to the bridge," Margraves said, listing slightly to starboard as he walked. "Offered him a drink, but he didn't want one."

"All right," Branch said.

"He was bursting with questions," Margraves continued, chuckling to himself. "One of those earnest, tanned State Department men, out to win the war in five minutes flat. Very friendly boy. Wanted to know why I, personally, thought the fleet had been maneuvering in space for a year with no action."

"What did you tell him?"

"Said we were waiting for a consignment of zap guns," Margraves said. "I think he almost believed me. Then he started talking about logistics."

"Hm-m-m," Branch said. There was no telling what Margraves, half drunk, had told the representative. Not that it mattered. An official inquiry into the prosecution of the war had been due for a long time.

"I'm going to leave you here," Margraves said. "I've got some unfinished business to attend to."

"Right," Branch said, since it was all he could say. He knew that Margraves' unfinished business concerned a bottle.

He walked alone to the bridge.

The President's representative was looking at the huge location screen. It covered one entire wall, glowing with a slowly shifting pattern of dots. The thousands of green dots on the left represented the Earth fleet, separated by a black void from the orange of the enemy. As he watched, the fluid, three-dimensional front slowly changed. The armies of dots clustered, shifted, retreated, advanced, moving with hypnotic slowness.

But the black void remained between them. General Branch had been watching that sight for almost a year. As far as he was concerned, the screen was a luxury. He couldn't determine from it what was really happening. Only the CPC calculators could, and they didn't need it.

"How do you do, General Branch?" the President's representative said, coming forward and offering his hand. "My name's Richard Ellsner."

Branch shook hands, noticing that Margraves' description had been pretty good. The representative was no more than thirty. His tan looked strange, after a year of pallid faces.

"My credentials," Ellsner said, handing Branch a sheaf of papers. The general skimmed through them, noting Ellsner's authorization as Presidential Voice in Space. A high honor for so young a man.

"How are things on Earth?" Branch asked, just to say something. He ushered Ellsner to a chair, and sat down himself.

"Tight," Ellsner said. "We've been stripping the planet bare of radioactives to keep your fleet operating. To say nothing

of the tremendous cost of shipping food, oxygen, spare parts, and all the other equipment you need to keep a fleet this size in the field."

"I know," Branch murmured, his broad face expressionless.

"I'd like to start right in with the president's complaints," Ellsner said with an apologetic little laugh. "Just to get them off my chest."

"Go right ahead," Branch said.

"Now then," Ellsner began, consulting a pocket notebook, "you've had the fleet in space for eleven months and seven days. Is that right?"

"Yes."

"During that time there have been light engagements, but no actual hostilities. You—and the enemy commander—have been content, evidently, to sniff each other like discontented dogs."

"I wouldn't use that analogy," Branch said, conceiving an instant dislike for the young man. "But go on."

"I apologize. It was an unfortunate, though inevitable, comparison. Anyhow, there has been no battle, even though you have a numerical superiority. Is that correct?"

"Yes."

"And you know the maintenance of this fleet strains the resources of Earth. The President would like to know why battle has not been joined?"

"I'd like to hear the rest of the complaints first," Branch said. He tightened his battered fists, but, with remarkable self-control, kept them at his sides.

"Very well. The morale factor. We keep getting reports from you on the incidence of combat fatigue—crack-up, in plain language. The figures are absurd! Thirty per cent of your men seem to be under restraint. That's way out of line, even for a tense situation."

Branch didn't answer.

"To cut this short," Ellsner said, "I would like the answer to those questions. Then, I would like your assistance in negotiating a truce. This war was absurd to begin with. It was none of Earth's choosing. It seems to the President that, in view of the static situation, the enemy commander will be amenable to the idea."

Colonel Margraves staggered in, his face flushed. He had completed his unfinished business; adding another fourth to his half-drunk.

"What's this I hear about a truce?" he shouted.

Ellsner stared at him for a moment, then turned back to Branch.

"I suppose you will take care of this yourself. If you will contact the enemy commander, I will try to come to terms with him."

"They aren't interested," Branch said.

"How do you know?"

"I've tried. I've been trying to negotiate a truce for six months now. They want complete capitulation."

"But that's absurd," Ellsner said, shaking his head. "They have no bargaining point. The fleets are of approximately the same size. There have been no major engagements yet. How can they—"

"Easily," Margraves roared, walking up to the representative and peering truculently in his face.

"General. This man is drunk." Ellsner got to his feet.

"Of course, you little idiot! Don't you understand yet? *The war is lost!* Completely, irrevocably."

Ellsner turned angrily to Branch. The general sighed and stood up.

"That's right, Ellsner. The war is lost and every man in the fleet knows it. That's what's wrong with the morale. We're just hanging here, waiting to be blasted out of existence."

The fleets shifted and weaved. Thousands of dots floated in space, in twisted, random patterns.

Seemingly random.

The patterns interlocked, opened and closed. Dynamically, delicately balanced, each configuration was a planned move on a hundred thousand mile front. The opposing dots shifted to meet the exigencies of the new pattern.

Where was the advantage? To the unskilled eye, a chess game is a meaningless array of pieces and positions. But to the players—the game may be already won or lost.

The mechanical players who moved the thousands of dots knew who had won—and who had lost.

"Now let's all relax," Branch said soothingly. "Margraves, mix us a couple of drinks. I'll explain everything." The colonel moved to a well-stocked cabinet in a corner of the room.

"I'm waiting," Ellsner said.

"First, a review. Do you remember when the war was declared, two years ago? Both sides subscribed to the Holmstead pact, not to bomb home planets. A rendezvous was arranged in space, for the fleets to meet."

"That's ancient history," Ellsner said.

"It has a point. Earth's fleet blasted off, grouped and went to the rendezvous." Branch cleared his throat.

"Do you know the CPC's? The Configuration-Probability-Calculators? They're like chess players, enormously extended. They arrange the fleet in an optimum attack-defense pattern, based on the configuration of the opposing fleet. So the first pattern was set."

"I don't see the need—" Ellsner started, but Margraves, returning with the drinks, interrupted him.

"Wait, my boy. Soon there will be a blinding light."

"When the fleets met, the CPC's calculated the probabilities of attack. They found we'd lose approximately eighty-seven per cent of our fleet, to sixty-five per cent of the enemy's. If they attacked, they'd lose seventy-nine per cent, to our sixty-four. That was the situation as it stood then. By extrapolation, their *optimum* attack pattern—at that time—would net them a forty-five per cent loss. Ours would have given us a seventy-two per cent loss."

"I don't know much about the CPC's," Ellsner confessed. "My field's psych." He sipped his drink, grimaced, and sipped again.

"Think of them as chess players," Branch said. "They can estimate the loss probabilities for an attack at any given point of time, in any pattern. They can extrapolate the probable moves of both sides.

"That's why battle wasn't joined when we first met. No commander is going to annihilate his entire fleet like that."

"Well then," Ellsner said, "why haven't you exploited your slight numerical superiority? Why haven't you gotten an advantage over them?"

"Ah!" Margraves cried, sipping his drink. "It comes, the light!"

"Let me put it in the form of an analogy," Branch said. "If you have two chess players of equally high skill, the game's end is determined when one of them gains an advantage. Once the advantage is there, there's nothing the other player can do, unless the first makes a mistake. If everything goes as it should, the game's end is predetermined. The turning point may come a few moves after the game starts, although the game itself could drag on for hours."

"And remember," Margraves broke in, "to the casual eye, there may be no apparent advantage. Not a piece may have been lost."

"That's what's happened here," Branch finished sadly. "The CPC units in both fleets are of maximum efficiency. But the enemy has an edge, which they are carefully exploiting. And there's nothing we can do about it."

"But how did this happen?" Ellsner asked. "Who slipped up?"

"The CPC's have inducted the cause of the failure," Branch said. "The end of the war was inherent *in our take-off formation.*"

"What do you mean?" Ellsner said, setting down his drink.

"Just that. The configuration the fleet was in, light-years away from battle, before we had even contacted their fleet. When the two met, they had an infinitesimal advantage of position. That was enough. Enough for the CPC's, anyhow."

"If it's any consolation," Margraves put in, "it was a fifty-fifty chance. It could have just as well been us with the edge."

"I'll have to find out more about this," Ellsner said. "I don't understand it all yet."

Branch snarled: "The war's lost. What more do you want to know?"

Ellsner shook his head.

"Wilt snare me with predestination 'round," Margraves quoted, "and then impute my fall to sin?"

Lieutenant Nielson sat in front of the gunfire panel, his fingers interlocked. This was necessary, because Nielson had an almost overpowering desire to push the buttons.

The pretty buttons.

Then he swore, and sat on his hands. He had promised General Branch that he would carry on, and that was important. It was three days since he had seen the general, but he was determined to carry on. Resolutely he fixed his gaze on the gunfire dials.

Delicate indicators wavered and trembled. Dials measured distance, and adjusted aperture to range. The slender indicators rose and fell as the ship maneuvered, lifting toward the red line, but never quite reaching it.

The red line marked emergency. That was when he would start firing, when the little black arrow crossed the little red line.

He had been waiting almost a year now, for that little

arrow. Little arrow. Little narrow. Little arrow. Little narrow.
Stop it.

That was when he would start firing.

Lieutenant Nielson lifted his hands into view and inspected
his nails. Fastidiously he cleaned a bit of dirt out of one.
He interlocked his fingers again, and looked at the pretty
buttons, the black arrow, the red line.

He smiled to himself. He had promised the general. Only
three days ago.

So he pretended not to hear what the buttons were whis-
pering to him.

"The thing I don't see," Ellsner said, "is why you can't do
something about the pattern? Retreat and regroup, for example?"

"I'll explain that," Margraves said. "It'll give Ed a chance
for a drink. Come over here." He led Ellsner to an instrument panel. They had been showing Ellsner around the ship
for three days, more to relieve their own tension than for
any other reason. The last day had turned into a fairly pro-
longed drinking bout.

"Do you see this dial?" Margraves pointed to one. The
instrument panel covered an area four feet wide by twenty
feet long. The buttons and switches on it controlled the movements of the entire fleet.

"Notice the shaded area. That marks the safety limit. If
we use a forbidden configuration, the indicator goes over
and all hell breaks loose."

"And what is a forbidden configuration?"

Margraves thought for a moment. "The forbidden configurations are those which would give the enemy an attack
advantage. Or, to put it in another way, moves which change
the attack-probability-loss picture sufficiently to warrant an
attack."

"So you can move only within strict limits?" Ellsner asked,
looking at the dial.

"That's right. Out of the infinite number of possible formations, we can use only a few, if we want to play safe. It's
like chess. Say you'd like to put a sixth row pawn in your
opponent's back row. But it would take two moves to do it.
And after you move to the seventh row, your opponent has
a clear avenue, leading inevitably to checkmate.

"Of course, if the enemy advances too boldly the odds are
changed again, and *we* attack."

"That's our only hope," General Branch said. "We're praying they do something wrong. The fleet is in readiness for instant attack, if our CPC shows that the enemy has over-extended himself anywhere."

"And that's the reason for the crack-ups," Ellsner said. "Every man in the fleet on nerves' edge, waiting for a chance he's sure will never come. But having to wait anyhow. How long will this go on?"

"This moving and checking can go on for a little over two years," Branch said. "Then they will be in the optimum formation for attack, with a twenty-eight per cent loss probability to our ninety-three. They'll have to attack then, or the probabilities will start to shift back in our favor."

"You poor devils," Ellsner said softly. "Waiting for a chance that's never going to come. Knowing you're going to be blasted out of space sooner or later."

"Oh, it's jolly," said Margraves, with an instinctive dislike for a civilian's sympathy.

Something buzzed on the switchboard, and Branch walked over and plugged in a line. "Hello? Yes. Yes. . . . All right, Williams. Right." He unplugged the line.

"Colonel Williams has had to lock his men in their rooms," Branch said. "That's the third time this month. I'll have to get CPC to dope out a formation so we can take him out of the front." He walked to a side panel and started pushing buttons.

"And there it is," Margraves said. "What do you plan to do, Mr. Presidential Representative?"

The glittering dots shifted and deployed, advanced and retreated, always keeping a barrier of black space between them. The mechanical chess players watched each move, calculating its effect into the far future. Back and forth across the great chess board the pieces moved.

The chess players worked dispassionately, knowing beforehand the outcome of the game. In their strictly ordered universe there was no possible fluctuation, no stupidity, no failure.

They moved. And knew. And moved.

"Oh, yes," Lieutenant Nielson said to the smiling room. "Oh, yes." And look at all the buttons, he thought, laughing to himself.

So stupid. Georgia.

Nielson accepted the deep blue of sanctity, draping it across his shoulders. Bird song, somewhere.

Of course.

Three buttons red. He pushed them. Three buttons green. He pushed them. Four dials. Riverread.

"Oh-oh. Nielson's cracked."

"Three is for me," Nielson said, and touched his forehead with greatest stealth. Then he reached for the keyboard again. Unimaginable associations raced through his mind, produced by unaccountable stimuli.

"Better grab him. Watch out!"

Gentle hands surround me as I push two are brown for which is for mother, and one is high for all rest.

"Stop him from shooting off those guns!"

I am lifted into the air, I fly, I fly.

"Is there any hope for that man?" Ellsner asked, after they had locked Nielson in a ward.

"Who knows," Branch said. His broad face tightened; knots of muscle pushed out his cheeks. Suddenly he turned, shouted, and swung his fist wildly at the metal wall. After it hit, he grunted and grinned sheepishly.

"Silly, isn't it? Margraves drinks. I let off steam by hitting walls. Let's go eat."

The officers ate separate from the crew. Branch had found that some officers tended to get murdered by psychotic crewmen. It was best to keep them apart.

During the meal, Branch suddenly turned to Ellsner.

"Boy, I haven't told you the entire truth. I said this would go on for two years? Well, the men won't last that long. I don't know if I can hold this fleet together for two more weeks."

"What would you suggest?"

"I don't know," Branch said. He still refused to consider surrender, although he knew it was the only realistic answer.

"I'm not sure," Ellsner said, "but I think there may be a way out of your dilemma." The officers stopped eating and looked at him.

"Have you got some superweapons for us?" Margraves asked. "A disintegrator strapped to your chest?"

"I'm afraid not. But I think you've been so close to the situation that you don't see it in its true light. A case of the forest for the trees."

"Go on," Branch said, munching methodically on a piece of bread.

"Consider the universe as the CPC sees it. A world of strict causality. A logical, coherent universe. In this world, every effect has a cause. Every factor can be instantly accounted for.

"That's not a picture of the real world. There *is no* explanation for everything, really. The CPC is built to see a specialized universe, and to extrapolate on the basis of that."

"So," Margraves said, "what would you do?"

"Throw the world out of joint," Ellsner said. "Bring in uncertainty. Add a human factor that the machines can't calculate."

"How can you introduce uncertainty in a chess game?" Branch asked, interested in spite of himself.

"By sneezing at a crucial moment, perhaps. How could a machine calculate that?"

"It wouldn't have to. It would just classify it as extraneous noise, and ignore it."

"True." Ellsner thought for a moment. "This battle—how long will it take once the actual hostilities are begun?"

"About six minutes," Branch told him. "Plus or minus twenty seconds."

"That confirms an idea of mine," Ellsner said. "The chess game analogy you use is faulty. There's no real comparison."

"It's a convenient way of thinking of it," Margraves said.

"But it's an *untrue* way of thinking of it. Checkmating a king can't be equated with destroying a fleet. Nor is the rest of the situation like chess. In chess you play by rules previously agreed upon by the players. In this game you can make up your own rules."

"This game has inherent rules of its own," Branch said.

"No," Ellsner said. "Only the CPC's have rules. How about this? Suppose you dispensed with the CPC's? Gave every commander his head, told him to attack on his own, with no pattern. What would happen?"

"It wouldn't work," Margraves told him. "The CPC can still total the picture, on the basis of the planning ability of the average human. More than that, they can handle the attack of a few thousand second-rate calculators—humans—with ease. It would be like shooting clay pigeons."

"But you've *got* to try something," Ellsner pleaded.

"Now wait a minute," Branch said. "You can spout theory

all you want. I know what the CPC's tell me, and I believe them. I'm still in command of this fleet, and I'm not going to risk the lives in my command on some harebrained scheme."

"Harebrained schemes sometimes win wars," Ellsner said.

"They usually lose them."

"The war is lost already, by your own admission."

"I can still wait for them to make a mistake."

"Do you think it will come?"

"No."

"Well then?"

"I'm still going to wait."

The rest of the meal was completed in moody silence. Afterward, Ellsner went to his room.

"Well, Ed?" Margraves asked, unbuttoning his shirt.

"Well yourself," the general said. He lay down on his bed, trying not to think. It was too much. Logistics. Predetermined battles. The coming debacle. He considered slamming his fist against the wall, but decided against it. It was sprained already. He was going to sleep.

On the borderline between slumber and sleep, he heard a click.

The door!

Branch jumped out of bed and tried the knob. Then he threw himself against it.

Locked.

"General, please strap yourself down. We are attacking." It was Ellsner's voice, over the intercom.

"I looked over that keyboard of yours, sir, and found the magnetic doorlocks. Mighty handy in case of a mutiny, isn't it?"

"You idiot!" Branch shouted. "You'll kill us all! That CPC—"

"I've disconnected our CPC," Ellsner said pleasantly. "I'm a pretty logical boy, and I think I know how a sneeze will bother them."

"He's mad," Margraves shouted to Branch. Together they threw themselves against the metal door.

Then they were thrown to the floor.

"All gunners—fire at will!" Ellsner broadcasted to the fleet.

The ship was in motion. The attack was underway!

The dots drifted together, crossing the no man's land of space.

They coalesced! Energy flared, and the battle was joined.

Six minutes, human time. Hours for the electronically fast chess player. He checked his pieces for an instant, deducing the pattern of attack.

There was no pattern!

Half of the opposing chess player's pieces shot out into space, completely out of the battle. Whole flanks advanced, split, rejoined, wrenched forward, dissolved their formation, formed it again.

No pattern? There *had* to be a pattern. The chess player knew that everything had a pattern. It was just a question of finding it, of taking the moves already made and extrapolating to determine what the end was supposed to be.

The end was—chaos!

The dots swept in and out, shot away at right angles to the battle, checked and returned, meaninglessly.

What did it mean, the chess player asked himself with the calmness of metal. He waited for a recognizable configuration to emerge.

Watching dispassionately as his pieces were swept off the board.

"I'm letting you out of your room now," Ellsner called, "but don't try to stop me. I think I've won your battle."

The lock released. The two officers ran down the corridor to the bridge, determined to break Ellsner into little pieces.

Inside, they slowed down.

The screen showed the great mass of Earth dots sweeping over a scattering of enemy dots.

What stopped them, however, was Nielson, laughing, his hands sweeping over switches and buttons on the great master control board.

The CPC was droning the losses. "Earth—eighteen per cent. Enemy—eighty-three. Eighty-four. Eighty-six. Earth, nineteen per cent."

"Mate!" Ellsner shouted. He stood beside Nielson, a Stillson wrench clenched in his hand. "Lack of pattern. I gave their CPC something it couldn't handle. An attack with no apparent pattern. Meaningless configurations!"

"But what are they doing?" Branch asked, gesturing at the dwindling enemy dots.

"Still relying on their chess player," Ellsner said. "Still

waiting for him to dope out the attack pattern in this madman's mind. Too much faith in machines, general. This man doesn't even know he's precipitating an attack."

. . . And push three that's for dad on the olive tree I always wanted to two two two Danbury fair with buckle shoe brown all brown buttons down and in, sin, eight red for sin—

"What's the wrench for?" Margraves asked.

"That?" Ellsner weighed it in his hand. "That's to turn off Nielson here, after the attack."

. . . And five and love and black, all blacks, fair buttons in I remember when I was very young at all push five and there on the grass ouch—

SUBSISTENCE

LEVEL

HER mother had warned her. "Are you out of your mind, Amelia? Why in heaven's name must you marry a *pioneer?* How do you expect to be happy in a wilderness?"

"The Cap isn't a wilderness, Mother," Amelia had said.

"It isn't civilized. It's a crude, primitive place. And how long will this *pioneer* be satisfied there? I know the type. He'll always want some new place to conquer."

"Then I'll conquer it with him," Amelia had said, certain of her own pioneering spirit.

Her mother wasn't so sure. "Frontier life is hard, dear. Harder than you imagine. Are you really prepared to give up your friends, all the comforts you've known?"

"Yes!"

Her mother wanted to say more. But since her husband's death, she had become less certain of her own convictions, less determined to impose them on others.

"It's your life," she said at last.

"Don't worry, Mother, I know what I'm doing," Amelia said.

She knew that Dirk Bogren couldn't stand crowding. He was a big man and he needed elbow room, and silence, and free air to breathe. He had told her about his father, who had settled in the newly reclaimed Gobi Desert. It broke the old man's heart when the place got so crowded that land had to be fenced in according to county regulations and he died with his face turned toward the stars.

That was Dirk, too. She married him, and moved to the desolate Southern Polar Cap.

But settlers came after them, and soon the Cap was called Cap City, and then it had stores and factories, and neat little suburbs stretching across the atom-heated land.

It happened sooner than she ever expected.

One evening they were sitting on the veranda, and Dirk was looking over his land. He stared for a long time at the tip of a radar tower on a distant rise of the land.

"Getting crowded around here," he said finally.

"Yes, it is—a little," Amelia agreed.

"They'll be building a golf course next. Figure it's time to move on?"

"All right," Amelia said, after the slightest hesitation. And that was all that had to be said.

They sold their farm. They bought a second-hand spaceship and filled it with the barest necessities of life. The evening before blastoff, Dirk's friends threw a farewell party for him.

They were the old inhabitants and they could remember when the Cap was still partly ice and snow. They kidded Dirk, half enviously.

"Going to the asteroids, eh?"

"That's the place," Dirk said.

"But you're soft!" an old man cackled. "Easy living's got you, Dirk."

"Oh, I don't know."

"Think you can still work an honest five-hour day?"

Dirk grinned and drank his beer, and listened to the women give Amelia advice.

"Take *plenty* of warm things. *I remember on Mars*—"

"First-aid equipment—"

"The trouble with low gravity—"

"Dirk!" a man shouted. "You taking a pretty little thing like her to an *asteroid*?"

"Sure," Dirk said.

"She won't like it," another man warned. "No parties, no new clothes, no doodads."

"Folks go crazy from overwork out there."

"Don't you believe them," an older woman put in hastily. "You'll love it once you get used to it."

"I'm sure I will," Amelia said politely and hoped it was true.

Just before blastoff, she called her mother and told her the news.

Her mother wasn't surprised.

"Well, dear," she said, "it won't be easy. But you knew that before you married him. The asteroids—that's where your father wanted to go."

Amelia remembered her father as a gentle, soft-spoken man. Every night, when he returned from the bank, he would read through the ads for used spaceships and he would compile detailed lists of the equipment an explorer would need. Mother was dead set against any change and would not be moved. There were few open arguments, but a bitterness existed beneath the surface—until all bitterness was resolved when a helicopter smashed into her father's car one day, when he was returning from the bank.

"Try to be a good wife to him," her mother urged.

"Of course I will," Amelia declared a little angrily.

The new frontiers were in space, for Earth was tame and settled now. Dirk had studied the available charts of the Asteroid Belt, but they didn't tell him much. No one had ever penetrated very far and the vast extent was simply marked UNKNOWN TERRITORY.

It was a long journey and a dangerous one, but free land was there, land for the taking, and all the room a man could ask. Dirk fought through the shifting patterns of rock with steady patience. The spaceship was always pointed implacably outward, though no route was marked.

"We're not turning back," he told Amelia, "so there's no sense charting a way."

She nodded agreement, but her breath came short when she looked at the bleak, dead spots of light ahead. She couldn't help feeling apprehensive about their new life, the grim, lonely existence of the frontier. She shivered and put her hand over Dirk's.

He smiled, never taking his eyes off the dials.

They found a slab of rock several miles long by a mile wide. They landed on the dark, airless little world, set up their pressure dome and turned on the gravity. As soon as it approached normal, Dirk set to work uncrating the Control Robot. It was a long, tiring job, but finally he inserted the tape and activated the controls.

The robot went to work. Dirk turned on all available searchlights. Using the small crane, he lifted their Frontier Shelter out of the ship's hold, placed it near the center of the dome, and activated it. The Shelter opened like a gigantic flower, blossoming into a neat five-room dwelling, complete with basic furniture, kitchen, plumbing, and disposal units.

It was a start. But everything couldn't be unpacked at once. The temperature control was buried somewhere in the hold of the ship, and Dirk had to warm their house with an auxiliary heater hooked to the generator.

Amelia was too cold to make dinner. The temperature in the Shelter hovered around 52 degrees Fahrenheit. Even in her Explorers, Inc., furs, she was cold, and the dismal glow of the fluorescents made her feel colder.

"Dirk," she asked timidly, "couldn't you make it a little warmer?"

"I suppose I could, but that would slow down the robot."

"I didn't know," Amelia said. "I'll be all right."

But it was impossible working under fluorescents and she set the dial wrong on the Basic Ration Pack. The steak came out overdone, the potatoes were lumpy, and the chill was barely taken off the apple pie.

"I'm afraid I'm not much good at roughing it," Amelia said, trying to smile.

"Forget it," Dirk told her, and wolfed down his food as though it were regular Earthside fare.

They turned in. Amelia could hardly sleep on the emergency mattress. But she had the dubious satisfaction of knowing that Dirk was uncomfortable, too. He *had* been softened by the relatively easy life at the Cap.

When they awoke, everything seemed more cheerful. The Control Robot, working through the night, had set up the main lighting plant. Now they had their own little sun in the sky and a fair approximation of night and day. The Control had also unloaded the heavy Farm Robots, and they in turn had unloaded the Household Robots.

Dirk directed the topsoil manufacturing and coordinated the work of his robots as they force-seeded the soil. He worked a full five-hour day, and when the little sun was low on the horizon, he came home exhausted.

Amelia, meanwhile, had taped in her basic food sequences during the day, and that evening she was able to give her husband a plain but hearty eight-course dinner.

"Of course, it's not the twenty-plate special," she apologized as he munched on the hors d'oeuvres.

"Never could eat all that food, anyhow," Dirk said.

"And the wine isn't properly chilled."

Dirk looked up and grinned. "Hell, honey, I could drink warm Ola-Cola and never notice it."

"Not while *I'm* cook here," Amelia said. But she could see one advantage of frontier life already—a hungry man would eat anything that was put in front of him.

After helping Amelia pile the dishes into the washer, Dirk set up a projector in their living room. As a double feature flicked across the screen, they sat in durable foam-rubber chairs, just as generations of pioneers before them had done. This continuity with the past touched Amelia deeply.

And Dirk unpacked their regular bed and adjusted the gravity under it. That night they slept as soundly as they ever had at the Cap.

But the work on the asteroid was ceaseless and unremitting. Dirk labored five and, several times, even six hours a day with his Field Robots, changing tapes, bellowing commands, sweating to get the best out of them. In a few days, the force-seeded plants began to show green against the synthesized black loam. But it was apparent at once that it was a stunted crop.

Dirk's mouth tightened and he set his robots to pumping trace elements into the soil. He tinkered with his sun until he had increased its ultraviolet output. But the resulting crop, a week later, was a failure.

Amelia came out to the fields that day. Dirk's face was outlined by the garish sunset and his clenched fists were on his hips. He was staring at the poor, dwarfed, shoulder-high corn.

There was nothing Amelia could say. She put her hand comfortingly on his shoulder.

"We're not licked," Dirk muttered.

"What will you do?" Amelia asked.

"I'll plant a crop a week, if need be. I'll work the robots until their joints crystallize. This soil will yield. It must yield!"

Amelia stepped back, surprised at the vehemence of his tone. But she could understand how he felt. On Earth, a farmer simply gave the orders to his Control Robot, and in a few days he was ready to harvest. Dirk had been working and watching this miserable crop for over a week.

"What will you do with it?" she asked.

"Feed it to the animals," Dirk said contemptuously. They walked to the house together in the gathering twilight.

The next day, Dirk took his farm animals out of the freezers, reanimated them, and set up their pens and stalls. The beasts fed contentedly on the corn and wheat. Force-seeds went back into the ground—and the second growing was of normal size.

Amelia had little time to observe this triumph. Their five-room dwelling was small by Earth standards, but it still needed coordinating.

It was difficult. She had grown up in an ordinary suburban home, where the housekeeping duties were arranged in automatic time sequences. Here, each function was handled by an individual machine. There was no time to recess them into the walls and they were forever in the way, ruining her decor, making the house look like a machine shop.

Instead of a single, centralized switchboard, Amelia had dials, buttons and switches everywhere, jury-rigged in casual style. At first, she had to spend a large part of each day just hunting for the proper controls for dry-cleaning, floor-scrubbing, window-washing, and other necessities she had taken for granted at home. Dirk had promised to hook all the circuits together, but he was always busy with his own work.

Her House Robots were impossible. They were frontier models, built for durability, with none of the refinements she had known. Their memories were poor and they could anticipate nothing. At the end of the day, Amelia's ears would ring from their harsh, raucous voices. And most of the time her house looked as though the robots had been attacking it, instead of cleaning it.

The long five-hour days of drudgery went on and on, until Amelia felt she couldn't take any more of it. In desperation, she called her mother on the tele-circuit.

In the tiny, streaked screen, she could see her mother sitting in her favorite pneumo-chair beside the polarized glass wall. It was adjusted for vision now, and Amelia could see the city in the distance, springing upward in its glistening beauty.

"What seems to be wrong?" her mother asked.

A robot glided behind her mother's chair and noiselessly put down a cup of tea. Amelia was sure that no command had been given. The sensitive mechanical had anticipated her, the way Earth robots did after long acquaintance with a family.

"Well, it's—" Amelia began to explain almost hysterically.

Her own robot lurched through the room, almost breaking down a door when the photo-electric circuit didn't respond quickly enough. It was too much.

"I want to come home!" Amelia cried.

"You know you're always welcome, dear. But what about your husband?"

"Dirk will come, I'm sure of it. We can find him a good job, can't we, Mother?"

"I suppose so. But is that what he wants?"

"What?" Amelia asked blankly.

"Will a man like that be satisfied on Earth? Will he return?"

"He will if he loves me."

"Do you love him?"

"Mother, that's unfair!" Amelia said, feeling a little sick inside.

"It's a mistake to make a man do something he doesn't want to do," her mother told her. "Your father . . . Anyhow, don't you think you could make it work?"

"I don't know," Amelia said. "I guess—I guess I'll try."

Things did get better after that. Amelia learned how to live with her home, to overlook its inconveniences. She could see that someday it might be as pleasant as they had eventually made their farm on the Cap.

But they had left the Cap. And as soon as this place was livable, Dirk would want to move on, into a fresh wilderness.

One day, Dirk found her sitting beside their tiny swimming pool, weeping hopelessly.

"Hey!" he said. "What's wrong?"

"Nothing."

Clumsily he stroked her hair. "Tell me."

"Nothing, nothing."

"*Tell me.*"

"Oh, it's all the work of making a nice home and putting up curtains and training the robots and everything, and knowing—"

"Knowing what?"

"That someday you'll want to move on and it'll all be for nothing." She sat up and tried to smile. "I'm sorry, Dirk. I shouldn't have mentioned it."

Dirk thought for a long time. Then he looked at her closely, and said, "I want to make you happy. You believe that, don't you?"

She nodded.

"I guess we've done enough moving around. This is our home. We'll stay right here."

"Really, Dirk?"

"It's a promise."

She hugged him tightly. Then she remembered. "Good heavens! My Napoleons will be ruined!" She ran off to the kitchen.

The next weeks were the happiest Amelia had ever known. In the morning, their pre-set sun burst into glory, waking them to the morning chores. After they had a hearty breakfast, the work of the day began.

It was never dull. One day Amelia and Dirk might erect a meteor screen to reinforce their pressure dome. Or they might tinker with the wind machine, to help the reanimated bees provide better pollination for the crops.

In the evenings, they had their sunsets. Sometimes Dirk would have the Field Robots stage a clumsy dance. He was a firm but understanding master. He believed that a little variety was good for robots as well as for humans.

Amelia regretted Earth only once. That was when Dirk picked up a Lunar rebroadcast of the Easter Parade on their television set. The music and bright colors made Amelia's heart ache—but it was only for a moment.

Their first visitor came several months later in a gaily decorated spaceship that settled on Dirk's rough-hewn landing field. Painted on its side in letters eight feet high was the sign POTTER'S TRAVELING STORE. A dapper young man climbed out, sniffed the atmosphere, wrinkled his nose, and walked up to the house.

"What can I do for you, stranger?" Dirk asked at the door.

"Good day, countryman. I'm Potter," the young man said, extending his hand which Dirk did not shake. "I was making my usual swing around Mars when I heard about you folks out here. Thought you might like to buy a few gimcracks to—to brighten up the place."

"Don't want a thing," Dirk said.

Potter grinned amiably, but he had seen the severe, undecorated farmhouse and the spartan swimming pool.

"Something for the wife?" Potter asked, winking at Amelia. "I won't be around this way for a while."

"Glad to hear it," Dirk said.

But Amelia, her eyes glowing, wanted to go through Potter's whole stock, and she dragged Dirk along.

Like a child, she tried out all the household appliances, the modern time-saving gadgets for the home. She looked longingly at the dresses—dainty, sheer, with automatic necklines and hems—and thought of her own drab tailored fashions.

But then she saw the Acting Robots. With their amazingly human appearance and civilized mannerisms, they reminded her poignantly of home.

"Couldn't we buy a troupe?" she asked Dirk.

"We've got the movies, haven't we? They were good enough for my father—"

"But, Dirk, these robots put on real plays!"

"This particular troupe puts on all hit plays clear back to George Bernard Shaw," Potter told them.

Dirk looked with distaste at the handsome humanoid machines. "What else do they do?"

"Do? They act," Potter said. "Good Lord, countryman, you wouldn't expect a work of art to do farm labor, would you?"

"Why not?" Dirk asked. "I don't believe in pampering robots. Farm labor's good enough for my Control Robot and I'll bet he's smarter than these gimcracks."

"Your Control Robot is not an artist," Potter said loftily.

Amelia was so wistful that Dirk bought the troupe. While he was lugging them to the house—Acting Robots were too delicate to walk over stony ground—Amelia bought a dress.

"What's a girl like you doing in this wilderness?" Potter asked.

"I like it."

"Oh, it's livable, I suppose. Life of toil, doing without luxuries, advancing the frontier, all that sort of thing. But don't you get sick of roughing it?"

Amelia didn't answer him.

Potter shrugged his shoulders. "Well," he said, "this sector's ripe for colonization. You'll be having company before long."

Amelia took her dress and returned to the house. Potter blasted off.

Dirk was forced to admit the Acting Robots made pleasant company during the long, still evenings. He even became quite fond of *Man and Superman*. After a while, he began to give the robots acting directions, which they naturally ignored.

Still, he was always certain that his Control Robot could do as well, if the voice box were only improved a little.

Amusements, however, were swallowed in the long five-hour working days. Dirk began to collect other little asteroids and grapple them to his original claim. He force-planted a forest, constructed a waterfall, and tinkered with his father's old climate machine.

Finally he got it working and was able to reproduce seasons on their planetoid.

One day, the tele-circuit spluttered into life and Dirk received a spacegram. It was from Explorers, Inc., an Earth firm that manufactured a complete line of equipment for pioneers. They offered Dirk a job as head of their main testing laboratory, at a salary just a little short of stupendous.

"Oh, Dirk!" Amelia gasped. "What an opportunity!"

"Opportunity? What are you talking about?"

"You could be wealthy. You could have anything you wanted."

"I've got what I want," Dirk said. "Tell them no, thanks."

Amelia sighed wearily. She cabled Dirk's refusal to the firm—but added that his services might possibly be available later.

After all, there was no sense in completely shutting the door.

During the long summer, another spaceship swung over Dirk's landing field. This one was older and even more battered than Dirk's, and it dropped the last five feet to the ground, jarring the whole small planetoid. A young couple staggered out, on the point of collapse.

They were Jean and Percy Phillips, who had homesteaded several thousand miles from Dirk's holdings. Everything had gone wrong. Their power had failed, their robots had broken down, their food had run out. In desperation, they had set out for Dirk's farm. They were near starvation, having been without food for almost two whole days.

Dirk and Amelia gave them the hospitality of the frontier and quickly nursed them back to health. It became readily apparent that the Phillipses were ignorant of any of the rules of survival.

Percy Phillips didn't even know how to handle robots. Dirk had to explain it to him.

"You have to show them who's boss," Dirk said.

"But I should think that the proper command, given in a low, pleasant voice—"

"Not out here," Dirk said, with a positive shake of his head. "These Work Robots are a stupid, unresponsive lot. They're sullen and resentful. You have to *pound* the commands into them. Kick them, if need be."

Phillips raised both eyebrows. "Mistreat a robot?"

"You have to show them who the human is."

"But in Colonization School, we were taught to treat our robots with dignity," Phillips protested.

"You'll lose a lot of Earth notions out here," Dirk said bluntly. "Now listen to me. I was raised by robots. Some of my best friends are robots. I know what I'm talking about. The only way they'll show you any respect is if you make them."

Phillips admitted doubtfully that Dirk might be right.

"Of course I'm right!" Dirk stated. "You say your power supply failed?"

"Yes, but the robots didn't—"

"Didn't they? They have access to the charge outlets, haven't they?"

"Of course. When they're low, they recharge themselves."

"You think they stop when they're full? A robot'll keep on drawing power until it's all gone. Haven't you learned that old robot stunt?"

"I guess that's what happened," Phillips said. "But why would they do it?"

"Robots are congenital drunks," Dirk told him. "The manufacturers stamp it into them. That way, they burn out faster and you have to buy more robots. Believe me, you'll be doing them a favor if you keep them power-starved."

"I guess I've got a lot to learn," Phillips sighed.

And Jean, his wife, had even more to learn. Amelia had to show her over and over again that buttons won't push themselves, switches won't close without timing circuits, and dials won't leap of their own free will to the proper setting, Cleaning Robots can't be trusted with the cooking, and the Rub-A-Tub, although a versatile instrument, *won't* put up the preserves.

"I never thought there was so much to it," Jean said. "How do you do it all?"

"You'll learn," Amelia assured her, remembering her own early days on the frontier.

The Phillipses set out again for their claim. Amelia had thought it would be lonely when they were gone, but it was pleasant to be alone with Dirk again, to get back to work on their farm.

But people wouldn't leave them alone. Next, a man from Mars Rural Power called. Homesteaders were moving into the Asteroid Belt, he explained, so the power outlets were being extended. He wanted to hook up Dirk's farm to the Mars Power tight-beam network.

"Nope," Dirk said.

"Why not? It's not expensive—"

"I make my own power."

"Oh, these little generators," the man said, looking scornfully at Dirk's sun. "But for really high-gain performance—"

"Don't need it. This farm runs fast enough to suit me."

"You could get more work out of your robots."

"Just wear them out faster."

"Then you could get the latest models."

"The new ones just burn out faster."

"A better generating system, then," the man said. "That little sun of yours doesn't have much of an output."

"Puts out enough to satisfy me."

The man shook his head wonderingly. "I guess I'll never understand you pioneers," he said, and left.

They tried to resume their life. But lights were beginning to wink on from neighboring asteroids, and the Lunar television was jammed with local signals. The mail rocket began to make weekly stops and a travel bureau started trips into the Belt.

The familiar, dissatisfied look came over Dirk's face. He studied the sky around him. It was closing in. He was losing his elbow room, and the silence of his farm was broken by the flame of passing rockets.

But he had promised Amelia and he was going to keep that promise if it killed him. His face grew gaunt and he began to work six, seven—sometimes actually eight—hours a day.

A sewing machine salesman called, and a bright, determined woman tried to sell Dirk the Solar Encyclopedia. The ship routes were established now and the long, dangerous trail had become a superhighway.

One night, while Dirk and Amelia were sitting on their porch, they saw an immense sign light up the sky. It stretched over miles of space, and read: ROSEN'S SHOPPING CENTER. STORES, RESTAURANT, BEST DRINKS IN THE ASTEROIDS.

"Stores," Amelia murmured. "And a restaurant! Oh, Dirk, couldn't we go?"

"Why not?" he said, with a helpless shrug of his shoulders.

The next day, Amelia put on her new dress and made Dirk wear his one custom-tailored suit. They got into the old spaceship and set out.

Rosen's Center, a bustling frontier town sprawling across four linked asteroids, was struggling valiantly to become a city. Already driftways had been installed on all the streets. The town was filled with noisy, eager people, and robots clumped down the ways, loaded with gear.

Amelia took Dirk into a restaurant, where they were served a real Earthside dinner. Dirk didn't enjoy it. He was slightly nauseous from breathing other people's air and the food was too delicate to stick to one's ribs. The meal ended with Dirk ordering the wrong wine and trying to tip the robot waiter.

Thoroughly miserable, he allowed himself to be dragged from one store to another. The only time he showed any interest was when they entered a heavy-tools shop.

He examined a new anti-gravity engine. It was a model he had never seen.

"Just the thing for canceling heavy-planet effects," the robot clerk told him. "We believe this machine would work splendidly on the moons of Jupiter, for example."

"The moons of Jupiter?"

"Just an example, sir," the robot said. "No one's ever been there. It's completely unexplored territory."

Dirk nodded absently, rubbing his hand along the machine's burnished surface.

"Look, Amelia," he said. "Do you suppose that job on Earth is still open?"

"It might be," she answered. "Why?"

"Might as well be on Earth as here. These people are playing at pioneering."

"Do you think you'd be happy on Earth?"

"Might."

"I doubt it," Amelia said. She was remembering how contented they had been on the asteroid. Their life had been full and complete, just the two of them, pushing back the wilderness with their rude tools—doing without—improvising.

That had been before people came, before Earth's noisy, elbowing civilization had crowded up to their doorstep.

Her mother had learned the hard way and had tried to tell her. Dirk would never be happy on Earth. And happiness for her was impossible if he fretted his life away as her father had, working on a job he hated and dreaming of another more satisfying one.

"We'll take the anti-grav engine," she told the robot. She turned to Dirk. "We'll need that out Jupiter way."

THE SLOW

SEASON

IF business had not been so slow, Slobold might not have done it. But business was slow. No one seemed to need the services of a ladies' custom tailor. Last month he had let his assistant go. Next month, he would have to let himself go.

Slobold was pondering this, surrounded by bolts of cotton, wool and gabardine, dusty pattern books and suited dummies, when the man walked in.

"You're Slobold?" the man asked.

"That's right, sir," Slobold said, jumping to his feet and straightening his vest.

"I'm Mr. Bellis. I suppose Klish has been in touch with you. About making the dresses."

Slobold thought rapidly, staring at the short, balding, fussily dressed man in front of him. He knew no one named Klish, so Mr. Bellis had the wrong tailor. He opened his mouth to tell him this. But then he remembered that business was very slow.

"Klish," he mused. "Oh yes, I believe so."

"I can tell you now," Mr. Bellis said sternly, "we will pay very well for the dresses. But we're exacting. Quite exacting."

"Of course, Mr. Bellis," Slobold said. He felt a slight tremor of guilt, but ignored it. Actually, he decided, he was doing Bellis a favor, since he was undoubtedly the best tailor named Slobold in the city. Later, if they discovered he was the wrong man, he could explain that he knew someone else named Klish.

"That's fine," Mr. Bellis said, stripping off his doeskin gloves. "Klish filled you in on the details, of course?"

Slobold didn't answer, but by means of a slow smile made it apparent that he knew and was amused.

"I daresay it came as quite a revelation," Mr. Bellis said. Slobold shrugged his shoulders.

"Well, you're a calm one," Bellis said admiringly. "But I suppose that's why Klish picked you."

Slobold busied himself lighting a cigar, since he didn't know what expression to assume.

"Now down to work," Mr. Bellis said briskly, slipping a hand into the breast pocket of his gray gabardine suit. "Here is the complete list of measurements for the first dress. There will be no fittings, naturally."

"Naturally," Slobold said.

"And we must have the completed article in three days. That is as long as Egrish can wait."

"Naturally," Slobold said again.

Mr. Bellis handed him the folded piece of paper. "Klish must have told you about the need for absolute secrecy, but let me repeat it. Nothing can slip out until the branch is well established. And here is your advance."

Slobold was so completely in control of himself that he didn't even wince at the sight of five crisp $100 bills.

"Three days," he said, tucking the money in his pocket.

Mr. Bellis stood for a moment, musing. Then he shrugged his shoulders and hurried out.

As soon as he was gone, Slobold unfolded the measurements. Since no one was watching, he allowed his jaw to gape open.

The dress was going to be like nothing ever before seen. It would fit an eight footer quite nicely, if she conformed to certain bodily modifications. But what modifications!

Reading through the 50 separate measurements and directions, Slobold realized that the wearer would have to have three breasts staggered across her stomach, each of a different size and shape. She would have a number of large bulges on her back. Only eight inches was allowed for her waist, but her four arms—to judge by the armholes—would be the thickness of young oak trees. There was no provision made for buttocks, but a flare was provided for tremendous thighs.

The material specified was cashmere. The color was to be jet black.

Slobold understood why there would be no fittings.

Staring at the directions, he gently tugged at his lower lip. "It's a costume," he said aloud, but shook his head. Costume specifications never included 50 separate measurements, and cashmere was not a suitable material.

He read the paper again, frowning deeply. Was it an expensive practical joke? That seemed dubious. Mr. Bellis had been too serious.

This dress, Slobold knew with every tailoring instinct, was being made for a person who fitted its dimensions.

That was a shivery thought. Although it was a bright day, Slobold switched on the overhead fluorescent lights.

He decided, tentatively, that it might be for a wealthy, but terribly deformed woman.

Except, he thought, that no one in the history of the world had ever been deformed like that.

But business was slow, and the price was right. If the price were right, he was willing to make dirndls for elephants and pinafores for hippopotamuses.

Therefore, shortly he retired to his back room, and, turning on every available light, began to draw patterns.

Three days later, Mr. Bellis returned.

"Excellent," he said, holding the dress in front of him. He pulled a tape measure out of his pocket and began to check off the measurements. "I don't doubt your work," he said, "but the garment must be form-fitting."

"Of course," Slobold said.

Mr. Bellis finished, and put away the tape. "That's just fine," he said. "Egrish will be pleased. The light was bothering her. None of them are used to it, you know."

"Ah," Slobold said.

"It's difficult, after spending all one's life in darkness. But they'll get acclimated."

"I should imagine so," Slobold said.

"And pretty soon they can begin work," Mr. Bellis said, with a complacent smile.

Slobold began to wrap the dress, his mind racing, trying to make some sense out of Bellis' words. *After spending one's life in darkness*, he thought, as he tucked in the tissue paper. *Getting acclimated*, he told himself, closing the box.

And Egrish wasn't the only one. Bellis had spoken of others. For the first time, Slobold considered the possibility that Egrish and the rest weren't from Earth. Could they be from Mars? No, plenty of light there. But how about the dark side of the moon?

"And here are the measurements for three other dresses," Mr. Bellis said.

"I can work from the ones you gave me," Slobold said, still thinking of other planets.

"How can you?" Mr. Bellis asked. "The others can't wear anything that would fit Egrish."

"Oh, I forgot," Slobold said, forcing his attention back. "Would Egrish like some more dresses out of the same pattern?"

"No. What for?"

Slobold closed his mouth tightly. Bellis might get suspicious if he made any more errors.

He looked over the new measurements.

Now he needed all his self-control, for these were as different from Egrish as Egrish had been from the human norm.

"Could you have these ready in a week?" Mr. Bellis asked. "I hate to rush you, but I want to get the branch established as soon as possible."

"A week? I think so," Slobold said, looking at the $100 bills that Bellis was fanning across the counter. "Yes, I'm quite sure I can."

"Fine," Mr. Bellis said. "The poor things just can't stand light."

"Why didn't they bring their clothes with them?" Slobold asked, and immediately wished he hadn't.

"What clothes?" Mr. Bellis asked, frowning at Slobold. "They don't have any clothes. Never had. And in a little while, they never will again."

"I forgot," Slobold said, perspiring freely.

"Well, a week then. And that will just about do it." Mr. Bellis walked to the door. "By the way," he said, "Klish will be back in a day or two from Darkside."

And with that he was gone.

Slobold worked feverishly that week. He kept his store lights burning at all hours, and avoided dark corners. Making the dresses told him what their wearers looked like, and that didn't help him sleep nights. He devoutly wished Bellis hadn't told him anything, for he knew too much for his peace of mind.

He knew that Egrish and her fellows lived their lives in darkness. That implied that they came from a lightless world.

What world?

And normally they didn't wear anything. Why did they need dresses now?

What were they? Why were they coming here? And what did Bellis mean about getting them to work?

Slobold decided that genteel starvation was better than employment of this sort.

"Egrish was quite pleased," Mr. Bellis said, a week later. He finished checking the measurements. "The others will be too, I'm sure."

"I'm glad to hear it," Slobold said.

"They're really more adaptable than I dared hope," Mr. Bellis said. "They're getting acclimated already. And, of course, your work will help."

"I'm very glad," Slobold said, smiling mechanically and wishing Bellis would leave.

But Bellis was feeling conversational. He leaned on the counter and said, "After all, there's no reason why they should function only in the darkness. It's very confining. That's why I brought them up from Darkside."

Slobold nodded.

"I think that's all," Bellis said, tucking the dress box under his arm. He started toward the door. "By the way," he said. "You should have told me that you were the wrong Slobold."

Slobold could only grin foolishly.

"But there'll be no damage done," Bellis said. "Since Egrish wants to thank you in person."

He closed the door gently behind him.

Slobold stood for a long time, staring at the door. Then he touched the $100 bills in his pocket.

"This is ridiculous," he told himself. Quickly he locked the front door. Then he hurried to the back door, and bolted it. Then he lighted a cigar.

"Perfectly ridiculous," he said. Outside it was broad daylight. He smiled at his fears, and snapped on the overhead lights.

He heard a soft noise behind him.

The cigar slid from his fingers, but Slobold didn't move. He didn't make a sound, although every nerve in his body was shrieking.

"Hello, Mr. Slobold," a voice said.

Slobold still was unable to move, there in his brightly lighted shop.

"We want to thank you for your very fine work," the voice said. "All of us."

Slobold knew that he would go crazy at once, if he *didn't* look. There could be nothing worse than *not* looking. Slowly, inexorably, he began to turn.

"Klish said we could come," the voice said. "Klish said you would be the first to see us. In the daytime, I mean."

Slobold completed his turn and looked. There was Egrish, and there were the others. They weren't wearing the dresses. *They weren't wearing the dresses.* How could they, when they had no bodies? Four gigantic heads floated in front of him. Heads? Yes, he supposed that the misshapen, bulging things were heads.

There was something vaguely familiar about them.

For a moment, Slobold tried desperately to convince himself that he was having an hallucination. He couldn't have met them before, he told himself. Bellis said they came from Darkside. They lived and worked in the dark. They had never owned clothes, never would again. . . .

Then Slobold remembered. He had met them once before, in a particularly bad dream.

They were nightmares.

Perfectly understandable, he thought crazily. Long overdue, really, when one comes to think about it. No reason why nightmares should restrict themselves to the night. Daytime—huge, undeveloped area, ripe for exploitation.

Mr. Bellis had started a daymare branch, and here they were.

But why dresses? Slobold knew, then, what he had been making, and it was just too much. His mind began to shiver and tremble, and warp around the edges. He wished he could go decently insane.

"We'll go now," Egrish said. "The light still bothers us."

Slobold saw the fantastic heads drift closer.

"Thank you for the sleeping masks. They fit perfectly."

Slobold collapsed to the floor.

"You'll be seeing us," Egrish said.

Alone at

Last

THE annual Io ship was already in blast position, and swarms of androids labored over the final ground details. A crowd had gathered to watch the event, to stand close together and be amused. Horns sounded, a warning siren began to shriek. Confetti poured from the last unsealed ports, and long silver and red streamers. From a loudspeaker came the hearty voice of the ship's captain—a human, of course—saying, "All ashore that's going ashore!"

In the midst of this joyous confusion stood Richard Arwell, perspiration pouring down his face, baggage heaped around him and more arriving every minute, barred from the ship by a ridiculous little government official.

"No, sir, I'm afraid I must refuse permission," the official was saying, with a certain unction.

Arwell's spacepass was signed and countersigned, his ticket was paid and vouchered. To reach this point he had waited at a hundred doors, explained himself to a hundred ignorant flunkies, and somehow won past them all. And now, at the very threshold of success, he was faced with failure.

"My papers are in order," Arwell pointed out, with a calmness he did not feel.

"They seem to be in order," the official said judiciously. "But your destination is so preposterous—"

At that moment a robot porter lumbered up with the packing case that contained Arwell's personal android.

"Careful with that," Arwell said.

The robot set it down with a resounding thud.

"Idiot!" Arwell screamed. "Incompetent fool!" He turned to the official. "Can't they ever build one that will follow orders properly?"

"That's what my wife asked me the other day," the official said, smiling sympathetically. "Just the other day our android—"

The robot said, "Put these on the ship, sir?"

"Not yet," the little official said.

The loudspeaker boomed, "Last call! All ashore!"

The official picked up Arwell's papers again. "Now then. This matter of destination. You really wish to go to an *asteroid*, sir?"

"Precisely," Arwell said. "I am going to live upon an asteroid, just as my papers state. If you would be good enough to sign them and let me aboard—"

"But no one lives on the asteroids," the official said. "There's no colony."

"I know."

"There isn't *anyone* on the asteroids!"

"True."

"You would be alone."

"I wish to be alone," Arwell said simply.

The official stared at him in disbelief. "But consider the risk. No one is alone today."

"I will be. As soon as you sign that paper," Arwell said. Looking toward the ship he saw that the ports were being sealed. "Please!"

The official hesitated. The papers were in order, true. But to be alone—to be completely alone—was dangerous, suicidal.

Still, it was undeniably legal.

He scrawled his name. Instantly Arwell shouted, "Porter, porter! Load these on the ship. Hurry! And be careful with the android!"

The porter lifted the case so abruptly that Arwell could hear the android's head slam against the side. He winced, but there was no time for a reprimand. The final port was closing.

"Wait!" Arwell screamed, and sprinted across the concrete apron, the robot porter thundering behind him. "Wait!" he screamed again, for a ship's android was methodically closing the port, oblivious to Arwell's unauthorized command. But a member of the human crew intervened, and the door's progress was arrested. Arwell sprinted inside, and the robot hurled his baggage after him. The port closed.

"Lie down!" the human crew member shouted. "Strap yourself. Drink this. We're lifting."

As the ship trembled and rose, Arwell felt a tremendous drunken satisfaction surge through him. He had made it, he had won, and soon, very soon, he would be alone!

But even in space, Arwell's troubles were not over. For the ship's captain, a tall, erect, graying man, decided not to put him on an asteroid.

"I simply cannot believe you know what you are doing," the captain said. "I beg you to reconsider."

They were sitting in upholstered chairs in the captain's comfortable lounge. Arwell felt unutterably weary, looking at the captain's smug, conventional face. Momentarily he considered strangling the man. But that would never bring him the solitude he desired. Somehow, he must convince this last dreary idiot.

A robot attendant glided noiselessly behind the captain. "Drink, sir?" it asked, in its sharp metallic voice. The captain jumped abruptly.

"*Must* you sneak up that way?" he asked the robot.

"Sorry, sir," the robot said. "Drink, sir?"

Both men accepted drinks. "Why," the captain mused, "can't these mechanicals be trained better?"

"I've often wondered that myself," Arwell said, with a knowing smile.

"This one," the captain went on, "is a perfectly efficient servitor. And yet, he does have that ridiculous habit of creeping up in back of people."

"My own android," Arwell said, "has a most annoying tremble in his left hand. Synaptic lag, I believe the technicians call it. One would think they could do something about it."

The captain shrugged. "Perhaps the new models . . . oh well." He sipped his drink.

Arwell sipped his own drink, and considered that an air of comradeship had been established. He had shown the captain that he was not a wild-eyed eccentric; on the contrary, that his ideas were quite conventional. Now was the time to press his advantage.

"I hope, sir," he said, "that we will have no difficulties about the asteroid."

The captain looked annoyed. "Mr. Arwell," he said, "you are asking me to do what is, essentially, an asocial act. To set you upon an asteroid would be a failure on my part as a human being. No one is alone in this day and age. We stay together. There is comfort in numbers, safety in quantity. We look after one another."

"Perfectly true," Arwell said. "But you must allow room for individual differences. I am one of those rare few who honestly desires solitude. This may make me unusual; but certainly my wishes are to be respected."

"Hmm." The captain looked earnestly at Arwell. "You *think* you desire solitude. But have you ever really experienced it?"

"No," Arwell admitted.

"Ah. Then you can have no conception of the dangers, the very real dangers inherent to that state. Wouldn't it be better, Mr. Arwell, to conform to the advantages of your day and age?"

The captain went on to speak of the Great Peace, which had now lasted over two hundred years, and of the psychological stability that was its basis. Slightly red in the face, he orated on the healthy mutual symbiosis between Man, that socially integrated animal, and his creature, the serene working mechanical. He spoke of Man's great task—the organization of the skills of his creatures.

"Quite true," Arwell said. "But not for me."

"Ah," the captain said, smiling wisely, "but have you tried? Have you experienced the thrill of cooperation? Directing the harvest androids as they toil over the wheat fields, guiding their labor under the seas—healthy, satisfying work. Even the lowliest of tasks—being a foreman over twenty or thirty factory robots, say—is not devoid of its sensation of solid accomplishment. And this sensation can be shared and augmented by contact with one's fellow humans."

"All that sort of thing is lacking in satisfaction for me," Arwell said. "It's just not for me. I want to spend the rest of my life alone, to read my books, to contemplate, to be on one tiny asteroid by myself."

The captain rubbed his eyes wearily. "Mr. Arwell," he said, "I believe you are sane, and therefore master of your destiny. I cannot stop you. But consider! Solitude is dangerous to modern man. Insidiously, implacably dangerous. For that reason he has learned to shun it."

"It will not be dangerous for me," Arwell said.

"I hope not," the captain said. "I sincerely hope not."

At last the orbit of Mars was passed, and the asteroid belt was reached. With the captain's help, Arwell picked out a good-sized chunk of rock. The ship matched velocities.

"You're sure you know what you're doing?" the captain asked.

"Positive!" Arwell said, barely able to contain his eagerness with his solitude so close at hand.

For the next few hours the helmeted crew transferred his gear from ship to asteroid and anchored it down. They set up his water producer and his air maker, and stowed his basic food components. At last they inflated the tough plastic bubble under which he would live, and proceeded to transfer his android.

"Careful with it," Arwell warned.

Suddenly the crate slipped through the clumsy gauntleted hands of a robot, and began to drift away.

"Get a line on that!" the captain shouted.

"Hurry!" Arwell screamed, watching his precious mechanical drift into the vacuum of space.

One of the human crew fired a line harpoon into the case and hauled it back, banging it roughly against the ship's side. With no further delay, the case was secured upon the asteroid. At last, Arwell was ready to take possession of his own little private world.

"I wish you would think about it," the captain said gravely. "The dangers of solitude—"

"Are all superstition," Arwell said abruptly, anxious to be alone. "There are no dangers."

"I will return with more provisions in six months," the captain said. "Believe me, there are dangers. It is no accident that modern man has avoided—"

"May I go now?" Arwell asked.

"Of course. And good luck," the captain said.

Spacesuited and helmeted, Arwell propelled himself to his tiny island in space, and from it watched the ship depart. When it became a dot of light no bigger than a star, he started to arrange his goods. First the android, of course. He hoped it wasn't bruised, after all the rough handling it had undergone. Quickly he opened the case and activated the mechanical. The forehead dial showed that energy was accumulating. Good enough.

He looked around. There was the asteroid, a lean black rock. There were his stores, his android, his food and water, his books. All around him was the immensity of space, the cold light of the stars, the faint sun, and the absolute black night.

He shuddered slightly and turned away.

His android was now activated. There was work to be done. But fascinated, he looked again into space.

The ship, that faint star, was gone from sight. For the first time, Arwell experienced what he had before only faintly imagined: solitude, perfect, complete and utter solitude. The merciless diamond points of the stars glared at him from the depths of a night that would never end. There was no human near him—for all he knew, the human race had ceased to exist. He was *alone*.

It was a situation that could drive a man insane.

Arwell loved it.

"Alone at last!" he shouted to the stars.

"Yes," said his android, lurching to its feet and advancing on him. "Alone at last."

FOREVER

WITH so much at stake, Charles Dennison should not have been careless. An inventor cannot afford carelessness, particularly when his invention is extremely valuable and obviously patentable. There are too many grasping hands ready to seize what belongs to someone else, too many men who feast upon the creativity of the innocent.

A touch of paranoia would have served Dennison well; but he was lacking in that vital characteristic of inventors. And he didn't even realize the full extent of his carelessness until a bullet, fired from a silenced weapon, chipped a granite wall not three inches from his head.

Then he knew. But by then it was too late.

Charles Dennison had been left a more than adequate income by his father. He had gone to Harvard, served a hitch in the Navy, then continued his education at M.I.T. Since the age of thirty-two, he had been engaged in private research, working in his own small laboratory in Riverdale, New York. Plant biology was his field. He published several noteworthy papers, and sold a new insecticide to a development corporation. The royalties helped him to expand his facilities.

Dennison enjoyed working alone. It suited his temperament, which was austere but not unfriendly. Two or three times a year, he would come to New York, see some plays and movies, and do a little serious drinking. He would then return gratefully to his seclusion. He was a bachelor and seemed destined to remain that way.

Not long after his fortieth birthday, Dennison stumbled across an intriguing clue which led him into a different branch of biology. He pursued his clue, developed it, extended it slowly into a hypothesis. After three more years, a lucky accident put the final proofs into his hands.

He had invented a most effective longevity drug. It was not proof against violence; aside from that, however, it could fairly be called an immortality serum.

Now was the time for caution. But years of seclusion had made Dennison unwary of people and their motives. He was more or less heedless of the world around him; it never occurred to him that the world was not equally heedless of him.

He thought only about his serum. It was valuable and patentable. But was it the sort of thing that should be revealed? Was the world ready for an immortality drug?

He had never enjoyed speculation of this sort. But since the atom bomb, many scientists had been forced to look at the ethics of their profession. Dennison looked at his and decided that immortality was inevitable.

Mankind had, throughout its existence, poked and probed into the recesses of nature, trying to figure out how things worked. If one man didn't discover fire, or the use of the lever, or gunpowder, or the atom bomb, or immortality, another would. Man willed to know all nature's secrets, and there was no way of keeping them hidden.

Armed with this bleak but comforting philosophy, Dennison packed his formulas and proofs into a briefcase, slipped a two-ounce bottle of the product into a jacket pocket, and left his Riverdale laboratory. It was already evening. He planned to spend the night in a good midtown hotel, see a movie, and proceed to the Patent Office in Washington the following day.

On the subway, Dennison was absorbed in a newspaper. He was barely conscious of the men sitting on either side of him. He became aware of them only when the man on his right poked him firmly in the ribs.

Dennison glanced over and saw the snub nose of a small automatic, concealed from the rest of the car by a newspaper, resting against his side.

"What is this?" Dennison asked.

"Hand it over," the man said.

Dennison was stunned. How could anyone have known

about his discovery? And how could they dare try to rob him in a public subway car?

Then he realized that they were probably just after his money.

"I don't have much on me," Dennison said hoarsely, reaching for his wallet.

The man on his left leaned over and slapped the briefcase. "Not money," he said. "The immortality stuff."

In some unaccountable fashion, they knew. What if he refused to give up his briefcase? Would they dare fire the automatic in the subway? It was a very small caliber weapon. Its noise might not even be heard above the subway's roar. And probably they felt justified in taking the risk for a prize as great as the one Dennison carried.

He looked at them quickly. They were mild-looking men, quietly, almost somberly dressed. Something about their clothing jogged Dennison's memory unpleasantly, but he didn't have time to place the recollection. The automatic was digging painfully into his ribs.

The subway was coming to a station. Dennison glanced at the man on his left and caught the glint of light on a tiny hypodermic.

Many inventors, involved only in their own thoughts, are slow of reaction. But Dennison had been a gunnery officer in the Navy and had seen his share of action. He was damned if he was going to give up his invention so easily.

He jumped from his seat and the hypo passed through the sleeve of his coat, just missing his arm. He swung the briefcase at the man with the automatic, catching him across the forehead with the metal edge. As the doors opened, he ran past a popeyed subway guard, up the stairs and into the street.

The two men followed, one of them streaming blood from his forehead. Dennison ran, looking wildly around for a policeman.

The men behind him were screaming, "Stop, thief! Police! Police! Stop that man!"

Apparently they were also prepared to face the police and to claim the briefcase and bottle as their own. Ridiculous! Yet the complete and indignant confidence in their shrill voices unnerved Dennison. He hated a scene.

Still, a policeman would be best. The briefcase was filled with proof of who he was. Even his name was initialed

on the outside of the briefcase. One glance would tell anyone . . .

He caught a flash of metal from his briefcase, and, still
running, looked at it. He was shocked to see a metal plate
fixed to the cowhide, over the place where his initials had
been. The man on his left must have done that when he
slapped the briefcase.

Dennison dug at the plate with his fingertips, but it would
not come off.

It read, *Property of Edward James Flaherty, Smithfield
Institute.*

Perhaps a policeman wouldn't be so much help, after all.

But the problem was academic, for Dennison saw no
policeman along the crowded Bronx street. People stood
aside as he ran past, staring open-mouthed, offering neither
assistance nor interference. But the men behind him were
still screaming, "Stop the thief! Stop the thief!"

The entire long block was alerted. The people, like some
sluggish beast goaded reluctantly into action, began to make
tentative movements toward Dennison, impelled by the out-
raged cries of his pursuers.

Unless he balanced the scales of public opinion, some do-
gooder was going to interfere soon. Dennison conquered his
shyness and pride, and called out, "Help me! They're trying
to rob me! Stop them!"

But his voice lacked the moral indignation, the absolute
conviction of his two shrill-voiced pursuers. A burly young
man stepped forward to block Dennison's way, but at the
last moment a woman pulled him back.

"Don't get into trouble, Charley."

"Why don't someone call a cop?"

"Yeah, where are the cops?"

"Over at a big fire on 178th Street, I hear."

"We oughta stop that guy."

"I'm willing if you're willing."

Dennison's way was suddenly blocked by four grinning
youths, teen-agers in black motorcycle jackets and boots,
excited by the chance for a little action, delighted at the
opportunity to hit someone in the name of law and order.

Dennison saw them, swerved suddenly and sprinted across
the street. A bus loomed in front of him.

He hurled himself out of its way, fell, got up again and
ran on.

His pursuers were delayed by the dense flow of traffic. Their high-pitched cries faded as Dennison turned into a side street, ran down its length, then down another.

He was in a section of massive apartment buildings. His lungs felt like a blast furnace and his left side seemed to be sewed together with red-hot wire. There was no help for it, he had to rest.

It was then that the first bullet, fired from a silenced weapon, chipped a granite wall not three inches from his head. That was when Dennison realized the full extent of his carelessness.

He pulled the bottle out of his pocket. He had hoped to carry out more experiments on the serum before trying it on human beings. Now there was no choice.

Dennison yanked out the stopper and drained the contents.

Immediately he was running again, as a second bullet scored the granite wall. The great blocks of apartments loomed endlessly ahead of him, silent and alien. There were no walkers upon the streets. There was only Dennison, running more slowly now past the immense, blank-faced apartments.

A long black car came up behind him, its searchlight probing into doors and alleys. Was it the police?

"That's him!" cried the shrill, unnerving voice of one of Dennison's pursuers.

Dennison ducked into a narrow alley between buildings, raced down it and into the next street.

There were two cars on that street, at either end of the block, their headlights shining toward each other, moving slowly to trap him in the middle. The alley gleamed with light now, from the first car's headlights shining down it. He was surrounded.

Dennison raced to the nearest apartment building and yanked at the door. It was locked. The two cars were almost even with him. And, looking at them, Dennison remembered the unpleasant jog his memory had given him earlier.

The two cars were hearses.

The men in the subway, with their solemn faces, solemn clothing, subdued neckties, shrill, indignant voices—they had reminded him of undertakers. They *had* been undertakers!

Of course! Of course! Oil companies might want to block

the invention of a cheap new fuel which could put them out of business; steel corporations might try to stop the development of an inexpensive, stronger-than-steel plastic . . .

And the production of an immortality serum would put the undertakers out of business.

His progress, and the progress of thousands of other researchers in biology, must have been watched. And when he made his discovery, they had been ready.

The hearses stopped, and somber-faced, respectable-looking men in black suits and pearl-gray neckties poured out and seized him. The briefcase was yanked out of his hand. He felt the prick of a needle in his shoulder. Then, with no transitional dizziness, he passed out.

He came to sitting in an armchair. There were armed men on either side of him. In front of him stood a small, plump, undistinguished-looking man in sedate clothing.

"My name is Mr. Bennet," the plump man said. "I wish to beg your forgiveness, Mr. Dennison, for the violence to which you were subjected. We found out about your invention only at the last moment and therefore had to improvise. The bullets were meant only to frighten and delay you. Murder was not our intention."

"You merely wanted to steal my discovery," Dennison said.

"Not at all," Mr. Bennet told him. "The secret of immortality has been in our possession for quite some time."

"I see. Then you want to keep immortality from the public in order to safeguard your damned undertaking business!"

"Isn't that rather a naive view?" Mr. Bennet asked, smiling. "As it happens, my associates and I are *not* undertakers. We took on the disguise in order to present an understandable motive if our plan to capture you had misfired. In that event, others would have believed exactly—and only —what you thought: that our purpose was to safeguard our business."

Dennison frowned and watchfully waited.

"Disguises come easily to us," Mr. Bennet said, still smiling. "Perhaps you have heard rumors about a new carburetor suppressed by the gasoline companies, or a new food source concealed by the great food suppliers, or a new synthetic hastily destroyed by the cotton-owning interests. That was us. And the inventions ended up here."

"You're trying to impress me," Dennison said.

"Certainly."

"Why did you stop me from patenting my immortality serum?"

"The world is not ready for it yet," said Mr. Bennet.

"It isn't ready for a lot of things," Dennison said. "Why didn't you block the atom bomb?"

"We tried, disguised as mercenary coal and oil interests. But we failed. However, we have succeeded with a surprising number of things."

"But what's the purpose behind it all?"

"Earth's welfare," Mr. Bennet said promptly. "Consider what would happen if the people were given your veritable immortality serum. The problems of birth rate, food production, living space all would be aggravated. Tensions would mount, war would be imminent—"

"So what?" Dennison challenged. "That's how things are right now, *without* immortality. Besides, there have been cries of doom about every new invention or discovery. Gunpowder, the printing press, nitroglycerine, the atom bomb, they were all supposed to destroy the race. But mankind has learned how to handle them. It had to! You can't turn back the clock, and you can't un-discover something. If it's there, mankind must deal with it!"

"Yes, in a bumbling, bloody, inefficient fashion," said Mr. Bennet, with an expression of distaste.

"Well, that's how Man is."

"Not if he's properly led," Mr. Bennet said.

"No?"

"Certainly not," said Mr. Bennet. "You see, the immortality serum provides a solution to the problem of political power. Rule by a permanent and enlightened elite is by far the best form of government; infinitely better than the blundering inefficiencies of democratic rule. But throughout history, this elite, whether monarchy, oligarchy, dictatorship or junta, has been unable to perpetuate itself. Leaders die, the followers squabble for power, and chaos is close behind. With immortality, this last flaw would be corrected. There would be no discontinuity of leadership, for the leaders would always be there."

"A permanent dictatorship," Dennison said.

"Yes. A permanent, benevolent rule by small, carefully chosen elite corps, based upon the sole and exclusive possession of immortality. It's historically inevitable. The only question is, who is going to get control first?"

"And you think you are?" Dennison demanded.

"Of course. Our organization is still small, but absolutely solid. It is bolstered by every new invention that comes into our hands and by every scientist who joins our ranks. Our time will come, Dennison! We'd like to have you with us, among the elite."

"You want *me* to join you?" Dennison asked, bewildered.

"We do. Our organization needs creative scientific minds to help us in our work, to help us save mankind from itself."

"Count me out," Dennison said, his heart beating fast.

"You won't join us?"

"I'd like to see you all hanged."

Mr. Bennet nodded thoughtfully and pursed his small lips. "You have taken your own serum, have you not?"

Dennison nodded. "I suppose that means you kill me now?"

"We don't kill," Mr. Bennet said. "We merely wait. I think you are a reasonable man, and I think you'll come to see things our way. We'll be around a long time. So will you. Take him away."

Dennison was led to an elevator that dropped deep into the Earth. He was marched down a long passageway lined with armed men. They went through four massive doors. At the fifth, Dennison was pushed inside alone, and the door was locked behind him.

He was in a large, well-furnished apartment. There were perhaps twenty people in the room, and they came forward to meet him.

One of them, a stocky, bearded man, was an old college acquaintance of Dennison's.

"Jim Ferris?"

"That's right," Ferris said. "Welcome to the Immortality Club, Dennison."

"I read you were killed in an air crash last year."

"I merely—disappeared," Ferris said, with a rueful smile, "after inventing the immortality serum. Just like the others."

"All of them?"

"Fifteen of the men here invented the serum independently. The rest are successful inventors in other fields. Our oldest member is Doctor Li, a serum discoverer, who disappeared from San Francisco in Nineteen-eleven. You are our latest acquisition. Our clubhouse is probably the most carefully guarded place on Earth."

Dennison said, "Nineteen-eleven!" Despair flooded him and

he sat down heavily in a chair. "Then there's no possibility of rescue?"

"None. There are only four choices available to us," Ferris said. "Some have left us and joined the Undertakers.

Others have suicided. A few have gone insane. The rest of us have formed the Immortality Club."

"What for?" Dennison bewilderedly asked.

"To get out of this place!" said Ferris. "To escape and give our discoveries to the world. To stop those hopeful little dictators upstairs."

"They must know what you're planning."

"Of course. But they let us live because, every so often, one of us gives up and joins them. And they don't think we can ever break out. They're much too smug. It's the basic defect of all power-elites, and their eventual undoing."

"You said this was the most closely guarded place on Earth?"

"It is," Ferris said.

"And some of you have been trying to break out for fifty years? Why, it'll take forever to escape!"

"Forever is exactly how long we have," said Ferris. "But we hope it won't take quite that long. Every new man brings new ideas, plans. One of them is bound to work."

"*Forever,*" Dennison said, his face buried in his hands.

"You can go back upstairs and join them," Ferris said, with a hard note to his voice, "or you can suicide, or just sit in a corner and go quietly mad. Take your pick."

Dennison looked up. "I must be honest with you and with myself. I don't think we can escape. Furthermore, I don't think any of you really believe we can."

Ferris shrugged his shoulders.

"Aside from that," Dennison said, "I think it's a damned good idea. If you'll bring me up to date, I'll contribute whatever I can to the Forever Project. And let's hope their complacency lasts."

"It will," Ferris said.

The escape did not take forever, of course. In one hundred and thirty-seven years, Dennison and his colleagues made their successful breakout and revealed the Undertakers' Plot. The Undertakers were tried before the High Court on charges of kidnapping, conspiracy to overthrow the government, and illegal possession of immortality. They were found guilty on all counts and summarily executed.

Dennison and his colleagues were also in illegal possession of immortality, which is the privilege only of our governmental elite. But the death penalty was waived in view of the Immortality Club's service to the State.

This mercy was premature, however. After some months the members of the Immortality Club went into hiding, with the avowed purpose of overthrowing the Elite Rule and disseminating immortality among the masses. Project Forever, as they termed it, has received some support from dissidents, who have not yet been apprehended. It cannot be considered a serious threat.

But this deviationist action in no way detracts from the glory of the Club's escape from the Undertakers. The ingenious way in which Dennison and his colleagues broke out of their seemingly impregnable prison, using only a steel belt buckle, a tungsten filament, three hens' eggs, and twelve chemicals that can be readily obtained from the human body, is too well known to be repeated here.

The Sweeper

of Loray

ABSOLUTELY impossible," declared Professor Carver.

"But I saw it," said Fred, his companion and bodyguard. "Late last night, I saw it! They carried in this hunter—he had his head half ripped off—and they—"

"Wait," Professor Carver said, leaning forward expectantly.

They had left their spaceship before dawn, in order to witness the sunrise ceremonies in the village of Loray, upon the planet of the same name. Sunrise ceremonies, viewed from a proper distance, are often colorful and can provide a whole chapter for an anthropologist's book; but Loray, as usual, proved a disappointment.

Without fanfare, the sun rose, in answer to prayers made to it the preceding night. Slowly it hoisted its dull red expanse above the horizon, warming the topmost branches of the great rain-forest that surrounded the village. And the natives slept on . . .

Not *all* the natives. Already the Sweeper was out, cleaning the debris between huts with his twig broom. He slowly shuffled along, human-shaped but unutterably alien. The Sweeper's face was a stylized blank, as though nature had drawn there a preliminary sketch of intelligent life. His head was strangely knobbed and his skin was pigmented a dirty gray.

The Sweeper sang to himself as he swept, in a thick, guttural voice. In only one way was the Sweeper distinguishable from his fellow Lorayans: painted across his face was a broad black band. This was his mark of station, the lowest possible station in that primitive society.

"Now then," Professor Carver said, after the sun had arisen without incident, "a phenomenon such as you describe could not exist. And it most especially could not exist upon a debased, scrubby little planet like this."

"I saw what I saw," Fred maintained. "I don't know from impossible, Professor. I saw it. You want to pass it up, that's up to you."

He leaned against the gnarly bole of a stabicus tree, folded his arms across his meager chest and glowered at the thatch-roofed village. They had been on Loray for nearly two months and Fred detested the village more each day.

He was an underweight, unlovely young man and he wore his hair in a bristling crewcut which accentuated the narrowness of his brow. He had accompanied the professor for close to ten years, had journeyed with him to dozens of planets, and had seen many strange and wonderful things. Everything he saw, however, only increased his contempt for the Galaxy at large. He desired only to return, wealthy and famous, or wealthy and unknown, to his home in Bayonne, New Jersey.

"This thing could make us rich," Fred accused. "And *you* want to pass it up."

Professsor Carver pursed his lips thoughtfully. Wealth was a pleasant thought, of course. But the professor didn't want to interrupt his important scientific work to engage in a wild goose chase. He was now completing his great book, the book that would fully amplify and document the thesis that he had put forth in his first paper, *Color Blindness Among the Thang Peoples*. He had expanded the thesis in his book, *Lack of Coordination in the Drang Race*. He had generalized it in his monumental *Intelligence Deficiencies Around the Galaxy*, in which he proved conclusively that intelligence among Non-Terrans decreases arithmetically as their planet's distance from Terra increases geometrically.

Now the thesis had come to full flower in Carver's most recent work, his unifying effort, which was to be titled *Underlying Causes of the Implicit Inferiority of Non-Terran Peoples*.

"If you're right—" Carver said.

"Look!" Fred cried. "They're bringing in another! See for yourself!"

Professor Carver hesitated. He was a portly, impressive, red-jowled man, given to slow and deliberate movement. He was dressed in a tropical explorer's uniform, although Loray was in a temperate zone. He carried a leather swagger stick, and strapped to his waist was a large revolver, a twin to the one Fred wore.

"If you're right," Carver said slowly, "it would indeed be, so to speak, a feather in the cap."

"Come on!" said Fred.

Four srag hunters were carrying a wounded companion to the medicine hut, and Carver and Fred fell in beside them. The hunters were visibly exhausted; they must have trekked for days to bring their friend to the village, for the srag hunts ranged deep into the rain-forest.

"Looks done for, huh?" Fred whispered.

Professor Carver nodded. Last month he had photographed a srag, from a vantage point very high in a very tall, stout tree. He knew it for a large, ill-tempered, quick-moving beast, with a dismaying array of claws, teeth and horns. It was also the only non-taboo meat-bearing animal on the planet. The natives had to kill srags or starve.

But the wounded man had not been quick enough with spear and shield, and the srag had opened him from throat to pelvis. The hunter had bled copiously, even though the wound had been hastily bound with dried grasses. Mercifully, he was unconscious.

"That chap hasn't a chance," Carver remarked. "It's a miracle he's stayed alive this long. Shock alone, to say nothing of the depth and extent of the wound—"

"You'll see," Fred said.

The village had suddenly come awake. Men and women, gray-skinned, knobby-headed, looked silently as the hunters marched toward the medicine hut. The Sweeper paused to watch. The village's only child stood before his parents' hut, and, thumb in mouth, stared at the procession. Deg, the medicine man, came out to meet the hunters, already wearing his ceremonial mask. The healing dancers assembled, quickly putting on their makeup.

"Think you can fix him, Doc?" Fred asked.

"One may hope," Deg replied piously.

They entered the dimly lighted medicine hut. The wounded Lorayan was laid tenderly upon a pallet of grasses and the dancers began to perform before him. Deg started a solemn chant.

"That'll never do it," Professor Carver pointed out to Fred, with the interested air of a man watching a steam shovel in operation. "Too late for faith healing. Listen to his breathing. Shallower, don't you think?"

"Absolutely," Fred said.

Deg finished his chant and bent over the wounded hunter. The Lorayan's breathing was labored. It slowed, hesitated . . .

"It is time!" cried the medicine man. He took a small wooden tube out of his pouch, uncorked it, and held it to the dying man's lips. The hunter drank. And then—

Carver blinked, and Fred grinned triumphantly. The hunter's breathing was becoming stronger. As they watched, the great gash became a line of scar tissue, then a thin pink mark, then an almost invisible white line.

The hunter sat up, scratched his head, grinned foolishly and asked for something to drink, preferably intoxicating.

Deg declared a festival on the spot.

Carver and Fred moved to the edge of the rain-forest for a conference. The professor walked like a man in a dream. His pendulous lower lip was thrust out and occasionally he shook his head.

"How about it?" Fred asked.

"It shouldn't be possible," said Carver dazedly. "No substance in nature should react like that. And you saw it work last night also?"

"Damned well right," Fred said. "They brought in this hunter—he had his head pulled half off. He swallowed some of that stuff and healed right before my eyes."

"Man's age-old dream," Carver mused. "A universal panacea!"

"We could get any price for stuff like that," Fred said.

"Yes, we could—as well as performing a duty to science," Professor Carver reminded him sternly. "Yes, Fred, I think we should obtain some of that substance."

They turned and, with firm strides, marched back to the village.

Dances were in progress, given by various members of the beast cults. At the moment, the Sathgohani, a cult representing a medium-sized deerlike animal, were performing. They could be recognized by the three red dots on their foreheads. Waiting their turn were the men of the Dresfeyxi and the Taganyes, cults representing other forest animals. The beasts adopted by the cults were taboo and there was an absolute injunction against their slaughter. Carver had been unable to discover the rationale behind this rule. The Lorayans refused to speak of it.

Deg, the medicine man, had removed his ceremonial mask. He was seated in front of his hut, watching the dancing. He arose when the Earthmen approached him.

"Peace!" he said.

"Sure," said Fred. "Nice job you did this morning."

Deg smiled modestly. "The gods answered our prayers."

"The gods?" said Carver. "It looked as though the serum did most of the work."

"Serum? Oh, the sersee juice!" Deg made a ceremonial gesture as he mentioned the name. "Yes, the sersee juice is the mother of the Lorayan people."

"We'd like to buy some," Fred said bluntly, ignoring Professor Carver's disapproving frown. "What would you take for a gallon?"

"I am sorry," Deg said.

"How about some nice beads? Mirrors? Or maybe a couple of steel knives?"

"It cannot be done," the medicine man asserted. "The sersee juice is sacred. It must be used only for holy healing."

"Don't hand me that," Fred said, a flush mounting his sallow cheek. "You gooks think you can—"

"We quite understand," Carver broke in smoothly. "We know about sacred things. Sacred things are sacred. They are not to be touched by profane hands."

"Are you crazy?" Fred whispered in English.

"You are a wise man," Deg said gravely. "You understand why I must refuse you."

"Of course. But it happens, Deg, I am a medicine man in my own country."

"Ah? I did not know this!"

"It is so. As a matter of fact, in my particular line, I am the highest medicine man."

"Then you must be a very holy man," Deg said, bowing his head.

"Man, he's holy!" Fred put in emphatically. "Holiest man you'll ever see around here."

"Please, Fred," Carver said, blinking modestly. He said to the medicine man, "It's true, although I don't like to hear about it. Under the circumstances, however, you can see that it would not be wrong to give me some sersee juice. On the contrary, it is your priestly duty to give me some."

The medicine man pondered for a long time while contrary emotions passed just barely perceptibly over his almost blank face. At last he said, "It may be so. Unfortunately, I cannot do what you require."

"Why not?"

"Because there is so little sersee juice, so terribly little. There is hardly enough for the village."

Deg smiled sadly and walked away.

Life in the village continued its simple, invariant way. The Sweeper moved slowly along, cleaning with his twig broom. The hunters trekked out in search of srags. The women of the village prepared food and looked after the village's one child. The priests and dancers prayed nightly for the sun to rise in the morning. Everyone was satisfied, in a humble, submissive fashion.

Everyone except the Earthmen.

They had more talks with Deg and slowly learned the complete story of the sersee juice and the troubles surrounding it.

The sersee bush was a small and sickly affair. It did not flourish in a state of nature. Yet it resisted cultivation and positively defied transplantation. The best one could do was to weed thoroughly around it and hope it would blossom. But most sersee bushes struggled for a year or two, then gave up the ghost. A few blossomed, and a few out of the few lived long enough to produce their characteristic red berries.

From the berry of the sersee bush was squeezed the elixir that meant life to the people of Loray.

"And you must remember," Deg pointed out, "how sparsely the sersee grows and how widely scattered it is. We must search for months, sometimes, to find a single bush with berries. And those berries will save the life of only a single Lorayan, or perhaps two at the most."

"Sad, very sad," Carver said. "But surely some form of intensive fertilization—"

"Everything has been tried."

"I realize," Carver said earnestly, "how important the sersee juice is to you. But if you could give us a little— even a pint or two—we could take it to Earth, have it examined, synthesized, perhaps. Then you could have all you need."

"But we dare not give any. Have you noticed how few children we have?"

Carver nodded.

"There are very few births. Our life is a constant struggle against the obliteration of our race. Every man's life must be preserved until there is a child to replace him. And this can be done only by our constant and never-ending search for the sersee berries. And there are never enough," the medicine man sighed. "Never enough."

"Does the juice cure *everything?*" Fred asked.

"It does more than that. Those who have tasted sersee add fifty of our years to their lives."

Carver opened his eyes wide. Fifty years on Loray was roughly the equivalent of sixty-three on Earth.

The sersee was more than a healing agent, more than a regenerator. It was a longevity drug as well.

He paused to consider the prospect of adding another sixty years to his lifetime. Then he asked, "What happens if a man takes sersee again after fifty years?"

"We do not know," Deg told him. "No man would take it a second time while there is not enough."

Carver and Fred exchanged glances.

"Now listen to me carefully, Deg," Professor Carver said. He spoke of the sacred duties of science. Science, he told the medicine man, was above race, above creed, above religion. The advancement of science was above life itself. What did it matter, after all, if a few more Lorayans died? They would die eventually anyhow. The important thing was for Terran science to have a sample of sersee.

"It may be as you say," Deg said. "But my choice is clear. As a priest of the Sunniheriat religion, I have a sacred trust to preserve the lives of my people. I cannot go against this trust."

He turned and walked off. The Earthmen frustratedly returned to their spaceship.

After coffee, Professor Carver opened a drawer and took out the manuscript of *Underlying Causes for the Implicit Inferiority of Non-Terran Races.* Lovingly he read over the last chapter, the chapter that dealt with the specialized inferiorities of the Lorayan people. Then he put the manuscript away.

"Almost finished, Fred," he told his assistant. "Another week's work, two weeks at the most!"

"Um," Fred replied, staring at the village through a porthole.

"This will do it," Carver said. "This book will prove, once and for all, the natural superiority of Terrans. We have proven it by force of arms, Fred, and we have proven it by our technology. Now it is proven by the impersonal processes of logic."

Fred nodded. He knew the professor was quoting from the book's introduction.

"Nothing must interfere with the great work," Carver said. "You agree with that, don't you?"

"Sure," Fred said absent-mindedly. "The book comes first. Put the gooks in their place."

"Well, I didn't exactly mean that. But you know what I mean. Under the circumstances, perhaps we should forget about sersee. Perhaps we should just finish the job we started."

Fred turned and faced his employer. "Professor, how much do you expect to make out of this book?"

"Hm? Well, the last did quite well, you will remember. This book should do even better. Ten, perhaps twenty thousand dollars!" He permitted himself a small smile. "I am fortunate, you see, in my subject matter. The general public of Earth seems to be rather interested in it, which is gratifying for a scientist."

"Say you even make fifty thousand. Chicken feed! Do you know what we could make on a test tube of sersee?"

"A hundred thousand?" Carver said vaguely.

"Are you kidding? Suppose a rich guy was dying and we had the only thing to cure him. He'd give everything he owned! Millions!"

"I believe you're right," Carver agreed. "And it *would* be a valuable scientific advancement. . . . But the medicine man unfortunately won't give us any."

"Buying isn't the only way." Fred unholstered his revolver and checked the chambers.

"I see, I see," Carver said, his red face turning slightly pale. "But have we the right?"

"What do *you* think?"

"Well, they *are* inferior. I believe I have proven that conclusively. You might indeed say that their lives don't weigh heavily in the scheme of things. Hm, yes—yes, Fred, we could save Terran lives with this!"

"We could save our own lives," Fred said. "Who wants to punk out ahead of time?"

Carver stood up and determinedly loosened his gun in its holster. "Remember," he told Fred, "we are doing this in the name of science, and for Earth."

"Absolutely, Professor," Fred said, moving toward the port, grinning.

They found Deg near the medicine hut. Carver said, without preamble, "We must have some sersee."

"But I explained to you," said the medicine man. "I told you why it was impossible."

"We gotta have it," Fred said. He pulled his revolver from its holster and looked ferociously at Deg.

"No."

"You think I'm kidding?" Fred asked. "You know what this weapon can do?"

"I have seen you use it."

"Maybe you think I won't use it on you."

"I do not care. You can have no sersee."

"I'll shoot," Fred warned, his voice rising angrily. "I swear to you, I'll shoot."

The villagers of Loray slowly gathered behind their medicine man. Gray-skinned, knobby-headed, they moved silently into position, the hunters carrying their spears, other villagers armed with knives and stones.

"You cannot have the sersee," Deg said.

Fred slowly leveled the revolver.

"Now, Fred," said Carver, "there's an awful lot of them. Do you really think—"

Fred's thin body tightened and his finger grew taut and white on the trigger. Carver closed his eyes.

There was a moment of dead silence. Then the revolver exploded. Carver warily opened his eyes.

The medicine man was still erect, although his knees were shaking. Fred was pulling back the hammer of the revolver. The villagers had made no sound. It was a moment before Carver could figure out what had happened. At last he saw the Sweeper.

The Sweeper lay on his face, his outstretched left hand still clutching his twig broom, his legs twitching feebly. Blood welled from the hole Fred had neatly drilled through his forehead.

Deg bent over the Sweeper, than straightened. "He is dead," the medicine man said.

"That's just the first," Fred warned, taking aim at a hunter.

"No!" cried Deg.

Fred looked at him with raised eyebrows.

"I will give it to you," Deg said. "I will give you all our sersee juice. Then you must go!"

He ran into the medicine hut and reappeared a moment later with three wooden tubes, which he thrust into Fred's hands.

"We're in business, Professor," Fred said. "Let's get moving!"

They walked past the silent villagers, toward their spaceship. Something bright flashed in the sunlight. Fred yipped and dropped his revolver. Professor Carver hastily scooped it up.

"One of those gooks cut me," Fred said. "Give me the revolver!"

A spear arced high and buried itself at their feet.

"Too many of them," said Carver. "Let's run for it!"

They sprinted to their ship with spears and knives singing around them, reached it safely and bolted the port.

"Too close," Carver said, panting for breath, leaning against the dogged port. "Have you got the serum?"

"I got it," said Fred, rubbing his arm. "Damn!"

"What's wrong?"

"My arm. It feels numb."

Carver examined the wound, pursed his lips thoughtfully, but made no comment.

"It's numb," Fred said. "I wonder if they poison those spears."

"It's quite possible," Professor Carver admitted.

"They did!" Fred shouted. "Look, the cut is changing color already!"

The edges of the wound had a blackened, septic look.

"Sulfa," Carver said. "Penicillin, too. I wouldn't worry much about it, Fred. Modern Terran drugs—"

"—might not even touch this stuff. Open one of those tubes!"

"But, Fred," Carver objected, "we have so little of it. Besides—"

"To hell with that," Fred said. He took one of the tubes and uncorked it with his teeth.

"Wait, Fred!"

"Wait, nothing!"

Fred drained the contents of the tube and flung it down. Carver said testily, "I was merely going to point out that the serum should be tested before an Earthman uses it. We don't know how it'll react on a human. It was for your own good."

"Sure it was," Fred said mockingly. "Just look at how the stuff is reacting."

The blackened wound had turned flesh-colored again and was sealing. Soon there was a line of white scar tissue. Then even that was gone, leaving firm pink flesh beneath.

"Pretty good, huh?" Fred gloated, with a slight touch of hysteria. "It works, Professor, it works! Drink one yourself, pal, live another sixty years. Do you suppose we can synthesize this stuff? Worth a million, worth ten million, worth a billion. And if we can't, there's always good old Loray. We can drop back every fifty years or so for a refill. The stuff even tastes good, Professor. Tastes like—what's wrong?"

Professor Carver was staring at Fred, his eyes wide with astonishment.

"What's the matter?" Fred asked, grinning. "Ain't my seams straight? What you staring at?"

Carver didn't answer. His mouth trembled. Slowly he backed away.

"What the hell is wrong!" Fred glared at Carver. Then he ran to the spaceship's head and looked in the mirror.

"What's happened to me?"

Carver tried to speak, but no words came. He watched as Fred's features slowly altered, smoothed, became blank, rudimentary, as though nature had drawn there a preliminary sketch of intelligent life. Strange knobs were coming out on Fred's head. His complexion was changing slowly from pink to gray.

"I told you to wait," Carver sighed.

"What's happening?" asked Fred in a frightened whimper.

"Well," Carver said, "it must all be residual in the sersee. The Lorayan birth-rate is practically non-existent, you know. Even with the sersee's healing powers, the race should have died out long ago. Unless the serum had another purpose as well—the ability to change lower animal forms into the Lorayan form."

"That's a wild guess!"

"A working hypothesis based upon Deg's statement that sersee is the mother of the Lorayan people. I'm afraid that is the true meaning of the beast cults and the reason they are taboo. The various beasts must be the origins of certain portions of the Lorayan people, perhaps all the Lorayan people. Even the topic is taboo; there clearly is a deep-seated sense of inferiority about their recent step up from bestiality."

Carver rubbed his forehead wearily. "The sersee juice has,"

he continued, "we may hazard, a role-sharing in terms of the life of the race. We may theorize—"

"To hell with theory," Fred said, and was horrified to find that his voice had grown thick and guttural, like a Lorayan voice. "Professor, do something!"

"There's nothing I can do."

"Maybe Terran science—"

"No, Fred," Carver said quietly.

"*What?*"

"Fred, please try to understand. I can't bring you back to earth."

"What do you mean? You must be crazy!"

"Not at all. How can I bring you back with such a fantastic story? They would consider the whole thing a gigantic hoax."

"But—"

"Listen to me. No one would believe! They would consider, rather, that you were an unusually intelligent Lorayan. Your very presence, Fred, would undermine the whole thesis of my book!"

"You can't leave me," Fred said. "You just can't do that."

Professor Carver still had both revolvers. He stuck one in his belt and leveled the other.

"I am not going to endanger the work of a lifetime. Get out, Fred."

"No!"

"I mean it. Get out, Fred."

"I won't! You'll have to shoot me!"

"I will if I must," Carver assured him. "I'll shoot you and throw you out."

He took aim. Fred backed to the port, undogged it, opened it. The villagers were waiting quietly outside.

"What will they do to me?"

"I'm really sorry, Fred," Carver said.

"I won't go!" Fred shrieked, gripping the edges of the port with both hands.

Carver shoved him into the waiting hands of the crowd and threw the remaining tubes of sersee after him. Then, quickly, not wishing to see what was going to happen, he sealed the port.

Within an hour, he was leaving the planet's atmospheric limits.

When he returned to Earth, his book, *Underlying Causes of the Implicit Inferiority of Non-Terran Peoples*, was hailed as a milestone in comparative anthropology. But he ran into some difficulty almost at once.

A space captain named Jones returned to Earth and maintained that, on the planet Loray, he had discovered a native who was in every significant way the equal of a Terran. And he had tape recordings and motion pictures to prove it.

Carver's thesis seemed in doubt for some time, until Carver examined the evidence for himself. Then he pointed out, with merciless logic, that the so-called super-Lorayan, this paragon of Loray, this supposed equal of Terran humanity, occupied the lowest position in the Lorayan hierarchy, the position of Sweeper, clearly shown by the broad black stripe across his face.

The space captain admitted that this was true.

Why then, Carver thundered, was this Lorayan Superior not able, in spite of his so-called abilities, to reach any higher position in the debased society in which he dwelt?

The question silenced the space captain and his supporters, demolished the entire school, as a matter of fact. And the Carverian Doctrine of the Implicit Inferiority of Non-Terrans is now accepted by reasoning Terrans everywhere in the Galaxy.

THE SPECIAL

EXHIBIT

THE Museum was unusually deserted that morning, Mr. Grant thought, as he led Mrs. Grant across the marble-floored lobby. Which was just as well, under the circumstances.

"Good morning, sir," said the red-cheeked old museum attendant.

"Good morning, Simmons," Mr. Grant said. "This is Mrs. Grant."

Mrs. Grant nodded sulkily, and leaned against a Central American war canoe. Her shoulders were on a level with those of the papier-mâché paddler; but broader by far. Looking at them, Mr. Grant wondered, for a moment, if the Special Exhibit would work. Could it succeed on a woman so large, so strong, so set in her ways.

He hoped so. Failure would be ridiculous.

"Welcome to our museum," the attendant said. "I believe this is the first time we've had the pleasure, Mrs. Grant."

"Haven't been here since I was a kid," Mrs. Grant said, stifling a yawn behind a large hand.

"Mrs. Grant is not particularly interested in the storied past," Mr. Grant explained, leaning on his cane. "My work in ornithology leaves her quite unimpressed. However, she has agreed to accompany me to the Special Exhibit."

"The *Special* Exhibit, sir?" the attendant asked. He consulted a notebook. "I don't believe—"

"Here is my invitation," Mr. Grant said.

"Yes, sir." The attendant examined the card carefully, then handed it back. "I hope you enjoy it, sir. The Special

149

Exhibit hasn't been shown often. I think that Dr. Carver and his wife were the last to view it."

"Of course," Mr. Grant said. He knew the mild, balding Carver quite well. And Carver's thin, nagging, red-haired wife was a good friend of Mrs. Grant. The Exhibit must have been effective, for Carver had been perceptibly more cheerful at work. The Special Exhibit was, of course, a far more effective problem solver than marriage counseling, psychiatry, psychoanalysis or even simple forbearance.

It was uniquely the Museum's project. The Museum liked to have its employees happy and contented, for only then could they serve Science properly. But aside from that, the Special Exhibit was educational, and filled a distinct gap in the Museum's program.

The general public had not been informed of it, for the general public was exceedingly conservative in the face of scientific necessity. But that was as it should be, Mr. Grant told himself.

The attendant fished a key from his pocket. "Be sure to return this to me, sir," he said.

Grant nodded, and led Mrs. Grant down the hall, past glass cases inhabited by Siberian tigers and giant pandas. A water buffalo stared glassy-eyed at them, and a family of Axis deer continued grazing in eternal peace.

"How long's this gonna take?" Mrs. Grant asked.

"Not long at all," Mr. Grant said, remembering that the Special Exhibit was noted for its swiftness.

"I've got some deliveries coming," Mrs. Grant said. "And some important things to do."

Leading her past a muntjac and a spotted chevrotian, Mr. Grant allowed himself to wonder, momentarily, what those important things might be. Mrs. Grant's interests seemed to center in television by day, and motion pictures by night.

Of course there *were* the deliveries.

Mr. Grant sighed. They were so obviously ill-matched. To think that he—a small, rather delicate fellow with a large mind—would voluntarily marry a woman of such heroic proportions and meager mentality. But it happened to others; Dr. Carver, for example.

Mr. Grant smiled wanly at the fiction of attracting opposites, at the entire romantic principle. Hadn't his work in ornithology taught him anything? Did the yellow-rumped Siskin mate with the condor? A single wild fling! How much better, he thought, if he had been content to join the French Foreign Legion, spend his inheritance in riotous living, or take to voodoo. Such ventures could, in time, be lived down. But marriage? Never. Not with Mrs. Grant as comfortable as she was.

Unless, of course, the Special Exhibit . . .

"This way," Mr. Grant murmured, leading her down an unexpected corridor concealed between glass cases.

"Where is this exhibit?" Mrs. Grant demanded. "I gotta be home for my deliveries."

"Just around here," Mr. Grant said, leading her past a door marked in red, No ADMITTANCE. He wondered about those deliveries. There seemed to be a tremendous number of them. And the delivery boy left a vile brand of cigar in the ash trays.

"Here we are," Mr. Grant said. He unlocked an iron door and walked into an immense room. The setting simulated a clearing in the jungle, and in front of them was a thatched hut. Behind that was a smaller hut, half hidden from view.

Several savages lounged on the vine-tangled ground, chattering at each other.

"They're alive!" Mrs. Grant exclaimed.

"Of course. This is, you see, a new experiment in descriptive anthropology."

To one side was an ancient wrinkled woman, adding wood to a fire that crackled under a large pot. Something was bubbling in the pot.

The warriors got to their feet when they noticed the Grants. One of them yawned and stretched, his muscles crackling.

"Magnificent fellows," Mrs. Grant whispered.

"Yes," Mr. Grant said. She *would* notice that.

Strewn around the ground in front of the first hut were decorated wooden swords, long, slender bows, sharp cane knives. And the room was filled with a continual background chirping. Breaking into it was a frenzied clucking. A bird honked angrily and something piped a reply.

Mrs. Grant said, "Can we go now—oh!"

One of the natives, wild and strange with his long coarse black hair and painted face, was standing beside her. Two others stood behind him. Looking at the group, Mr. Grant thought how savage Mrs. Grant really was, with her lavishly applied cosmetics, her fox skins and clanking jewelry.

"What do they want?" Mrs. Grant asked, eying the half-naked men with something less than fear.

"They'd like you to examine the village," Mr. Grant said. "It's part of the exhibit."

Mrs. Grant noticed that the first native was eying her with an admiring look and she allowed herself to be led forward.

She was shown the cooking pot, the weapons, the decorations on the first hut. Then the natives led her to the second hut, and one of them winked and beckoned her inside.

"Educational," she said, winking back, and followed him in. The other two natives entered, one picking up a cane knife before he went in.

"You didn't tell me they were supposed to be head hunters!" Mrs. Grant's voice floated faintly from the hut. "Have you seen all the shrunken heads?"

Mr. Grant nodded to himself. It was amazing, how hard those heads were to come by. The South American authorities had begun cracking down on their export. The Special Exhibit was, perhaps, the sole remaining source of this unique folk skill.

"One's got red hair. It looks just like Mrs.—"

There was a scream, and then the sound of a furious battle. Mr. Grant held his breath. There were three of them, to be sure, but Mrs. Grant was a very strong woman. Certainly she couldn't—

One of the natives came dancing out of the hut, and the hag by the fire picked up a few ominous instruments, and went inside. Whatever was in the pot continued to boil merrily.

Mr. Grant sighed with relief and decided that he had seen enough. After all, anthropology wasn't his line. He locked the iron door behind him and headed for the ornithology wing, deciding that Mrs. Grant's deliveries were not sufficiently important to require his presence.